THE MOTH
FOR THE STAR

by

James Reich

7.13 Books

ADVANCE PRAISE
FOR
THE MOTH FOR THE STAR

"An interrogation of the nature of evil set against the backdrop of a thrilling murder mystery, *The Moth for the Star*'s nuanced evocations of the beautiful and the damned accumulate in a terrifyingly relevant fiction, one that will keep you guessing to the last page and beyond."
—Jonathan Evison, author of *Small World*

"In *The Moth for the Star*, James Reich grips the reader from the first page and doesn't let go. Across sweeping landscapes and eras, from the 1929 market crash to post-apocalyptic environmental ruin, Reich builds a narrative storm that is menacing, inventive, and beautifully blade-sharp."
—Anne Valente, author of *Our Hearts Will Burn Us Down*

"Hypnotic, brooding, and ultimately spellbinding, *The Moth for the Star* is a marvel of psychological suspense rendered in prose as polished and shining as the novel's twin protagonists, who slice through space and time with the cold detachment of a steel razor."
—Chuck Greaves, author of *The Chimera Club*

"Every sentence on fire, James Reich's cosmopolitan orphic novel alchemizes mystery tropes into an existential exploration of uncertainty and unlearning that leaves time, space, love, yesterday, and tomorrow as energetically unsettled as a symphony of quantum strings."
—Lance Olsen, author of *Always Crashing in the Same Car: A Novel After David Bowie*

"A Depression-era murder ballad as sung by a high modernist, an amnesiac's love story as told by the Devil, *The Moth for the Star* is above all a sentence-by-sentence pleasure of maximalist prose used to hypnotically readable effect. Stunning and strange, Reich's latest whisks you up with the serious power of language into a compelling and utterly memorable world."

—**Constance E. Squires, author of** *Hit Your Brights* **and** *Along the Watchtower*

"*The Moth for the Star* is a triumph. It evokes the Depression era with a stylized, enervated elegance, and argues that the past is another planet: exotic, alien and inhospitable. The exquisite writing shines with diamond-cut brilliance, and the cumulative effect is uncanny, revealing a damaged world where reality has been fatally upended."

—**Simon Sellars, author of** *Applied Ballardianism: Memoir from a Parallel Universe* **and** *Code Beast*

PRAISE
FOR
JAMES REICH

"Somewhere between the macho-hipster fantasies of Quentin Tarantino and the banshee-activist theatrics of Pussy Riot...Now that's entertainment."
—*New York Times Book Review* on *Bombshell*

"Absolutely astonishing! Merciless in its refusal to pander to the easier implications of its material."
—**Barry Malzberg on** *The Song My Enemies Sing*

"In this exceptionally well-written novel, at times lyrical, elegiac, even mystical, James Reich asks some profound questions about time and identity."
—**Michael Moorcock on** *Soft Invasions*

"*Mistah Kurtz!* is not only satisfying because it reintroduces us to an adored classic, but because it takes us so convincingly someplace new. The deceit, longing, and mosquitos are so thick you'll grip your chair and slap at your ankles."
—**Ramona Ausubel, author of** *Awayland*

"It's an incredibly well-crafted, uniquely insightful book. Mr. Reich set himself a formidable task and he accomplished it with a masterful piece of fiction."
—**Malcolm McNeill on** *Mistah Kurtz! A Prelude to Heart of Darkness*

"James Reich writes like a demon."
—**Mary Dearborn, author of** *Ernest Hemingway, A Biography*

"You have to be strong to read this book. It rains fireballs."
—**Andrei Codrescu on** *I, Judas*

Printed in the United States of America

First Edition
1 2 3 4 5 6 7 8 9

Cover art by Alban Fischer
Edited by Kurt Baumeister

Library of Congress Cataloging-in-Publication Data

ISBN (paperback): 979-8-9877471-2-4
ISBN (eBook): 979-8-9877471-3-1
LCCN: 2023940655

PART ONE

"Every attentive person knows their Hell, but not all know their devil."
—Carl Jung, *Liber Novus*

CHAPTER ONE

FIVE YEARS LATER, CHARLES Varnas would recall the white linen against his shin, the shifting blade of his trousers, one knee folded across the other. How different was that sharp angle of flax in the Cairo breeze from the geometry of the shaving razor, dripping blood in his right hand? The razor was like an architect's tool, something an astrologer might employ, an astronomer's quadrant. All the clean angles of a murder—How agreeable it was to discover that as he reclined against the warm dune, he might align the cool material of his pant leg with the chrome yellow slant of the pyramids cutting the cloudless sky. He was, quite simply, a dark-haired man in a pale suit who had been on a long voyage. Across the mercury of that distance, he would remember this. They had struggled, he and the dead one beside him—the Adversary—cloven red as a sacrificial animal, its skin stiffening. The pulsing blood had suggested the bloom of amaranth. Charles Varnas reposed on that slope of sand, attentive to the heat of his breath, the approach of black, the welcome he gave his strange tears, and the infinite melancholy that would reach for him from the stars like a mob of brilliant spiders—

All of this returned to him again in the gasoline air of Lexington Avenue, at noon on the first Monday of September 1930, when a stray sheet of newsprint wrapped around his ankle. Like an awkward bird, Charles Varnas lifted his foot and plucked at the paper now fluttering against his shin, extending the tan briefcase that held his folding Smith Corona as a counterbalance at the edge of the sidewalk. He studied the page. It was from yesterday's *Times*. That drab Sunday had been witness to the sallow scrawl of breadlines, rain falling on long coats and declining furs boned with hunger. As he examined the newspaper sheet, between a story on air racing in Chicago, and what could be made of the laconic minutes saved by riding the trolley through the new system of traffic signals, something grandiose in the stray columns of type appealed to him. It insinuated like a rumor, whispering through his flesh as he stared at the headline: HOPES OF IMMORTALITY. With his briefcase pressed between his elbow and ribs, Varnas folded the newspaper page into a rectangular wad, slipping it into the breast pocket of his herringbone sports coat behind his leather notebook and his pen. Later, he would cut out the columns of the report that attracted him. For now, Varnas had some intuition to protect this omen that had come to push him back into his past. Lexington Avenue dissolved—

He was there again, with the pyramids under the desert twilight, the dune darkening with gore. He felt the slick oily coating of anise and fennel in his mouth as he watched the Pernod bottle rolling soundlessly away across the sand. He sensed the promise of evening, of a rendezvous when it was over. And there was the terrible corpse, faceless, indistinct under the greasy muslin of forgetting, witnessed through the narrowing aperture of his sorrow, all the hieroglyphs of violence. It had been Charles Varnas' twenty-fifth birthday, and his second visit to Egypt. Now, he was a murderer. Yet, he could not recall his victim in any detail, only the presence of a profound danger ebbing into the desert, to be borne away like someone drowning in the undulating sand. The true nature of the Adversary seemed to drift from his consciousness, and if he sought it with any aggressive attention, it merely evaded him more determinedly. It was as though some glamor of amnesia protected him, so that he could never give himself away. Who could confess what he did not recall? In a matter of hours, he would lose any sense of guilt at the act. It was necessary, after all, was it not? As he searched himself, it was, perhaps, the first moment of absolute confidence he had experienced. At last, he got to his feet. Unfamiliar constellations measured Varnas in their cool threads as he made his exit. The corpse would clot and sink, drawn under to vanish in those golden tenements of time.

Dipping his shaving razor into the silent surface of the desert, Varnas wiped the paste of blood and dust from the steel with his index finger and repeated this gesture until it was clean. In the future, he would be able to see his motions like a religious ritual, but now it felt like a childish preoccupation to make one thing perfect. He rubbed his finger and thumb together until the evidence vanished from the blade into his pores or was stripped and rolled into sticky pills against his skin. He had done the same with his seaweed colored mucous in childhood. Varnas' childhood had been constellated with cruelty, with figures set to hurt him, a sense of loss, and of being turned against what he loved.

He took out his handkerchief. There was time to polish the razor once more before closing and pocketing it. In the rising wind, he discarded the cloth, and lit a cigarette behind his cupped hand. He recalled walking carelessly back toward the suburbs of the city, sensing his shallow wake of footfalls being erased, the dunes enwrapping the body far behind him, sifting the blood down, lowering the heavy flesh, the bright bones, and its mask of disbelief into the slow waves of the desert. Infinitely, it would turn and fall into its vanishing.

It had seemed to Varnas that he walked for hours, one long howling street through Giza where the late trams rattled, the billboards peeled, and bare lightbulbs whined. This was the street he had first seen as a boy in 1912, with his father and mother. He removed his jacket, holding it in the crook of his arm like a matador's cape. The night air was cold against the Rorschach image at the division of his spine, his shirt becoming transparent, revealing something like a flesh-colored moth of sweat. Red embers and sweet cigarette smoke signaled the approach of scattered men, skimming him, quick as phantom children, their voices urgent and indecipherable. He was not afraid of them, as he might have been before, walking instead with a new killer's insouciance. A Suez Company oil drum burned between a crowd of brittle men in a side street. Sparks coiled upward into the darkness, then fell back. Down the street, a soldier slept in a raffia chair. In the moonlight, two others leaned against a blanketed camel, whispering over their revolvers in the animal's acrid shadow, nostalgic for the fighting of 1919. Varnas stepped between warm turrets of dung. He experienced a cool sense of being dispossessed. For now, those particular ghosts that harrowed him from abroad, from Oxford, Manchester, Niagara Falls, and the blear past of his Eastern European ancestors, they all declined from him, letting him almost alone. The ghosts were silent, confused by his determination, his dignity in victory.

Crossing the English Bridge and the Kobri El Gezira with its great bronze lions over the blackening Nile, he pulled his hip flask from his pocket and finished the gin he had saved for the return. Something was ascendent in him, vivid as a new star. Leaning on his elbows at the balustrade, he was midway across the bridge span. Varnas retrieved the razor from his other pocket, weighing it in his palm. The river was slow beneath him, assumed by the moon. It amused him that he could never look down from a vantage like this bridge or a tall building without imagining how it would be to jump. In the roadway at his back, a tubercular police motorcycle rasped, bearing its rider westward. He was alone. Without another thought, without opening it again, he let the razor fall into the Nile. Then, he slicked his black hair back from his eyes and walked on. It was late when he reached Ezbekiya where the white palm trunks stood like the pillars of a mausoleum. The killing was far behind him. It was all so distant that when he reached Khaled's Place with its exhausted cabaret, bad drinks, and impenetrable coffee, he could not recall why he had gone out that day—

In Manhattan now, blond-haired Charles Varnas walked briskly toward the Chrysler Building and his luncheon appointment. He had become quite used to the peroxide. It concealed his true nature, he thought, whatever that was. He did not care if, at times, the stark roots showed at his scalp. That had become his way of expressing something about which he was otherwise inarticulate. The sun came clutching and clawing between the tall buildings, as though it might snatch the weakest flesh off the street. Walking pleased him. Passing beneath the awnings and flags of the new Bloomingdale's, his slim form had flashed in the glass and the gloss of its facade. Those who might have encountered Varnas on that day at the beginning of September 1930 would have been struck by his flinty good looks, the blue eyes that squinted in his adopted American concentration always upon the future—eclipsing even his natural English disposition toward the past—the white crow's feet revealed by the flickering sunlight, that slight but perpetual tension in the jaw, and the grit of his teeth that came from too many escaped ideas, always just out of reach. Perhaps it was the pressure of keeping the past at bay. For, that day, the past inter-rupted, manipulated, and haunted his image of himself. Putting a finger to the thin scar beside his right eye, he wished he could have a drink, and wondered if he regretted coming home. Alcohol was still difficult to find.

At least, he thought, the metallic ministry of the Chrysler was some consolation. The most beautiful building in the world, it had been—fleetingly—the tallest. He strode under the entrance, an open sarcophagus of jet and aluminum, into the tobacco vault of the lobby. To Varnas, it suggested eternity, as though the great skyscraper had fused the future to the past in dreaming angles of marble, and gnostic light in golden pillars. The effect presented a space so strange that alchemists and aviators might repair in its elevators, their tomb doors inlaid with fanning papyrus leaves. Varnas did not care for Chrysler's automobiles, but the trappings of the man's wealth in this tower were luminous and magnificent, like the mad amber crypt of some new Akhenaton. When Varnas was a child, he had put a coin in his mouth and tasted the bitter blood taste of money. Now, like the shadow of a bird, pleasure passed over his features as he anticipated his ascent to the 66th floor and the Cloud Club.

Inside the elevator, he set down his briefcase and removed the folded page of newspaper from his breast pocket. He registered the narrow bite of sorrow that came as his fingers traced the ink. It reminded him of holding nettles as a boy. It was strange how much of his childhood interrupted him, of late. As much as he tried to live in the present, and to fix his version of the future in his mind, unpleasant recollections pressed upon him. He had tried to address his obsessive thoughts. Yes, he would say to himself, you have had that thought before. There is nothing to be gained by repeating it.

The news column that now compelled him like a curse concerned a Harvard lecture by a man named Robert Falconer, President of the University of Toronto. This man Falconer had declaimed on "The Idea of Immortality and Western Civilization." As the elevator rose, Varnas read how Falconer had spoken of the years before the War, and of the decline of the Christian spirit, such as it was, or whatever that was. Varnas was not a Christian. He was not certain what he was.

In the absence of any other image of Falconer, Varnas imagined him as a limpid, tortured Jesuit type. He superimposed a shovel-jawed photograph he had seen of the poet Gerard Manley Hopkins—*dapple-dawn-drawn Falcon, in his riding / Of the rolling level underneath him steady air*—in all the places where Falconer's name appeared. The poet Hopkins occupied one of the constellations of Varnas' being: the leather-bound notebook that Varnas kept at his breast contained pencil and ink transcriptions of Hopkins' poems.

The handwriting was not Varnas' own, but from someone he had known. Despite the barbed wire of the script and the bad memories, the poems transcended, somehow. He kept it deliberately close to his heart. There was space after the copies of Hopkins' poems for including his own on several blank pages. Despite himself, Varnas had not written a poem in many years. Perhaps he was doing Falconer a disservice with his imaginary physical comparison to Hopkins. Nevertheless, he thought, didn't all men cut the world to the limits of their own cloth? It did not hurt too much to admit that one's imagination was limited.

Images of the desert pulled at him. Perhaps keeping the poems was a mistake. Did they conspire with this stray newsprint that caught him in the street? Varnas winced, stiffened his legs, and studied the article. The *Times* recorded something of Falconer's lecture to his audience. Varnas read, "There were no clouds upon the hills, no mystery. In that atmosphere, men's faces lost their softer tones and their eyes grew keen. Material success affected them almost to elation. It was but a step from this into the sheer paganism that was frankly permitted to reign in the great cities of Western civilization."

Varnas wondered if this Falconer had lost money in the stock market. Hanging in the melancholy amber light of the elevator and ascending rapidly skyward as if in a dream of his own death, Varnas could only marvel at the smooth surfaces of this "sheer paganism," the gentle fingerprint on the golden console that selected the floors, and the ghosts of nicotine and pomade. Briefly, he imagined the elevator falling in its shaft. It must have felt that way last year if one had money of one's own. Varnas did not.

He was hungry, yet the hunger was pleasant evidence of being alive. It put him in touch with other people. Even the slight motion sickness he felt was reassuring. According to the newspaper article, Falconer had gone on to say that with all the sacrifices of the species to spirit and reason, it could only be reasonable that— even if the physical universe might not provide—some providential realm must surely exist for the more tender and faithful disciples of progress. He was talking about an everlasting afterlife, eternity in paradise. Would that logic—that life was simply so unbearable that there must be a Heaven—appeal to the breadlines? Had men considered this as gas drifted across the bloody trenches? It struck Varnas as naive. Immortality, he thought, was more arduous than that. Did immortality not contain its own hungers, its own agonies, sudden or eternal? Did not the hunger for being have its limits? Had not his own face come to appear lean and vicious, betraying the shortening rope of his existence and his desire for more? There were many reasons why a face might lose its softness, he thought, and not all of them material.

Varnas folded the paper and returned it to his breast pocket, fitting it carefully behind his notebook and pen. In time, he would write something new in the notebook. He might yet return to the talons and thorns of poetry—that which he had loved first and lost—and to the vision of himself like meat swung on a thread that he had hungered after. But, for the present, it contained only a pencil drawing he had made of a something like an awkward heron at the place where the copies of Hopkins' poems left off, its wings in gray lead spread on the creme paper, its beak too long. There was nothing after. He had drawn it weeks ago, and now it waited at his breast with a breathing inevitability. These things, he thought, collaborated. Time murmured obscenities.

CHAPTER TWO

FROM THE ELEVATOR, VARNAS strode to the upholstered doors that opened to the Cloud Club. Its oak-paneled roar poured like dirty gravel upon a coffin. Varnas scanned the room. Even through the obscurity of cigar smoke, the absence of women struck him immediately and unpleasantly. It always did. The men there talked of little that was not technical or bureaucratic. Easing through knots of dull conversation, he approached the crowded staircase. Men were discussing their businesses there, also. It struck him as being in bad taste, and tedious, but he was not certain what they should be talking about. The discovery of a new planet, perhaps. He had been thinking about it, intermittently, for months. Did it sustain life, this new and distant globe? What about the new DeMille, *Madam Satan*, with its orgy of costume parties on a doomed Zeppelin? What about life and death, fear versus courage, good versus evil, philosophy, sport, astrology, or speculations over anything but business? They should let women in, Varnas thought. Gripping the brass banister, experiencing himself sharply as an intruder, he ascended. Furtively, he scanned the charcoal and ivory murals of mechanics on the walls of bright carmine. At last, he came to the vaulted floor where Campbell waited.

Campbell, dressed in a crisp gray suit with a vivid peacock tie, was at their window table, nicotine-stained fingers drumming on the white linen cloth, blond hair slicked to one side. Three cigarettes had perished in a crystal ashtray. The restaurant was illuminated by futurist sconces like glowing fins on their dark granite columns. The walls and ceiling imitated the sky in airy artistic panels, with a vast painting of a jagged city breaking from a cloud bank occupying one wall, almost Biblical in its aspect. As he approached the table, Varnas gestured an ironic apology for being late. Sunlight flared against the silverware. Campbell was pulling another Lucky Strike from a silver cigarette holder when Varnas reached his seat, pushing his typewriter case beneath it.

Campbell took the water carafe in a pale, elegant hand and began pouring. "Here, Charles, have one of these."

Varnas spoke quietly, unfolding a napkin, noting a distilled faint of juniper from the glass, the atmosphere of alcohol burning at the rim like the corona of a transparent eclipse. "Gin? Oh, thank God." Silver embers scattered through him, bright as phosphor on a pin. The ice in his glass splintered pleasantly. There was a soft, expectant tremor in his fingers. "If I'd known you had gin, I might not have been late."

"But, if I'd told you, I couldn't have known if it was me or the booze that brought you."

Varnas imitated shock. "Darling..." The truth was that his ache for alcohol was ancient, archetypal. Something of his soul fluttered after it with a desire he found hard to articulate.

"Still, neither the police nor Ethyl Chaste—that's what I've decided to call the temperance ladies—will ever come up here."

Varnas drank again, a scintillating heat in his gums. "Poor bastards can't afford it," he said haughtily, bitterly. "Then again, neither can I."

"Do you like my hair?" Campbell said.

"Did you do something to it?"

"Swine." The aristocratic green of her eyes seemed to pulse once like a star glimpsed through stained glass.

"Yeah, I like it well enough," Varnas said. "It's short."

"Don't give me away."

"Of course not. I feel queer, though, Campbell."

"You bet you do." She made an obscene gesture with her cigarette and searched in her pocket for her lighter.

Varnas leaned across the table, his elbow settling into an empty bread plate. He glanced at the scene behind Campbell's padded angular shoulders, wreaths of smoke coiling about the noisy, suited tables, the men weaving like cobras in their seats, the waiters' jackets stiff as ancient ebony. Returning his gaze to hers, even in this androgynous disguise, she possessed the spectral radiance of a silent film. "It's really me who's in danger here," he said. "I'd like to bend you over."

"All in good time, Charles." Campbell lit her cigarette, snapping the lighter shut, and exhaling into Varnas' eyes, their English Channel blue enraptured under her shadowed breath. "All in good time."

Varnas coughed, lightly. "I don't see what's so good about time." He rested his temple against the cool pane of the window, unable to hear anything their waiter said when he arrived, merely gesturing his agreement with whatever Campbell ordered in that mannish voice she had cultivated to sustain her father's influence in forbidden places like this.

Manhattan spread out below them like an explosion, a metallic labyrinth of shrapnel and steam, fringed with piers that suggested the teeth of a warped cog. How long had Charles Varnas really been alive? He could not say. He did not believe in reincarnation, only that certain things, like the newspaper column coming to him on the street, suggested that he had more time than others. Somehow, he thought, he had not been born to die. He studied the thousands of men and women far below in the streets, submerged, bent, worn down by the malaise of falling money, walking under discolored Panama hats and sullen fedoras, women in cloche hats or headscarves, flecks of black faces down from

Harlem in slouch caps. They seemed to walk on quicksand, suspicious of the ground beneath them, the dark drag, and coils of panic beneath the straight sidewalk.

A year ago, the Crash had come almost on the solstice, chewing at the heels of Hallowe'en when the dead come in like animals from the fields to hunger at stiff doors and gray frosted windows. Now, it was conceivable that the city was the place of permanent phantoms under the advent of a plague. The bone men picked at the air and chattered over somber collars, cupping their cigarettes out of the cold waves of the season. He imagined lines of emaciated women leaning into the breeze, trailing shrouds of rotten silk and nooses of matted fox fur, gangs of diseased children vanishing into the sewers to form a vengeful militia. Campbell refilled his glass, and he drank with the pleasant desperation that the first glass always set in him. The waiter returned to their table. Christ, he thought, I feel alive.

"Well, it seems that they still have some caviar left in Heaven," Campbell said, dropping the menu and appraising her new haircut in the back of a spoon. Pomade left a thumbprint.

Varnas stared at her, possessed by her radiance.

She spoke to him in her natural voice. "An aphrodisiac, no less. Come on, Charles. Somewhere in the Caspian, some poor sturgeon has injured feelings. Eat up." The last time she had dressed this way, she had worn a short-clipped wig, but now it was real. Then, her longer blonde hair had been damp with perspiration when he removed it in the descending elevator. She had put a 37 mm shell casing in her underwear to petrify him when he unzipped her trousers. Campbell was unaware of her place above the world, and he almost despised her for that carelessness. Her father's sequestered money seemed to have gone almost untouched by the disaster, but they were working their way through it without caution. If Campbell had ever possessed an image of her luck, only the faintest ghost of that knowledge haunted her now. A glamor of arrogance or defiance hung on her. Her smile was firm with ancestral confidence. Sometimes, Varnas wondered if she really believed in herself as fervently as she appeared to. He pricked himself for being so charmed by it, for all that.

Campbell spoke absently, "Hmm, I should have kept some clippings to make a mustache." Then, in seriousness, "Say, have you seen the herons down in Battery Park? They're quite disgusting! I don't know where they came from—" Observing his reverie, she struck Varnas on the knuckles with her spoon.

"Christ! Lay off."

"I can't tell if you're bored, or tipsy, with your head lolling on your neck like that. Like a handsome corpse in a stream." Campbell smiled, lost in some sudden premonition into which the city collapsed. She offered him a cigarette and he took it, resisting the instinct to reach into his pocket for his lighter to assist her. She was one of the gentlemen. If he wanted to enjoy this afternoon, he would have to sustain the illusion.

The pain in Varnas' hand was sharp.

"I'm sorry," she said. "Really, I am."

Varnas finished his gin and poured another. The rapped hand was unsteady in the echo of pain, so that he spilled a few drops. "Okay. Sure, conversation: You've been to a seance, right?"

"I never miss one," she said. She made a show of passing Varnas a napkin so that she could caress the bones her silverware had injured beneath it. "Are you looking for any particular ghost?" The more direct she was, the better her chance of diverting him.

Varnas shook his head. "No, I believe rather that one is trying to find me." Yet, the place he sought for that confrontation was blank. He looked from the window again, feeling the familiar vertigo of dreaming, and falling. Once more, the desert forced itself upon him. He glimpsed two figures lying on a bloody dune. It was the view a hawk might have, an aerial view of the necropolis, the gloomy tide of Cairo against the emptiness, the tombs where Varnas stalked, candle-blind, the red sun hanging over a nightmare of sand. Disembodied, he saw himself.

Inside the elevator, unfastening the fly of her gray pants, Campbell said, "I remember making love between the paws of the Sphinx."

"You could help me remember, Campbell."

"My line is in helping you forget," she said, unironically. How long ago was it? She was not sure, even though it had only been five years. "No more talk of ghosts. We've only got sixty seconds before the lobby."

Varnas reached for her as the Chrysler rose around them. He pushed the button that halted the elevator, jealous of time.

On Lexington Avenue, they walked without touching. Campbell glanced back at the shining building and its ornaments. "Birds of prey, made of aluminum."

"Aren't we just?" Varnas said and hailed a Yellow Cab with his briefcase. The sky was dark. "Evening has come early," he said. "Get home, I don't want anything to rain on your pomade. I'll see you, Campbell." They made a play of shaking hands. Varnas laughed. "I'll take the next one, don't worry."

"It's sweet of you to carry the typewriter around. You really don't have to for my sake—only if it's useful to you. I just thought it might help—" Help us, Campbell had wanted to say. "I'm sorry that I hurt your hand."

"You're lucky it wasn't my typing hand."

Varnas did not immediately hail a cab for himself when Campbell had gone. Instead, he paced the crowded sidewalk aimlessly, glancing occasionally at the sky, troubled by his fractured memory and the surrounding obscurity. It reminded him of awakening confused from a night with too many drinks, when he could feel thousands of silvery molecules in his skull trying to boil the blindness away, when he was afraid of what he might have said or done. What, he wondered, must happen in that fissure between absence and remembrance, before what one dreads returns like the pop of a flashbulb in a darkened room? He felt as though he were rehearsing for a scene that would occur there, yet the circumstances he could not imagine. At last, he gave up.

The man who drove Varnas' cab wore a leather overcoat and a cap, a heavy oval medal with his license number. His driving gloves almost concealed his arthritis, but his fingers twisted around the wheel like briar. His face, reflected in the windshield, was that of a man trying not to scream, drowning beneath a silent sheet of ice. Such were the times, Varnas thought, since the money drained out of the world. His own money would be gone in another month, or before if he was not more cautious. Campbell wouldn't let him starve, but that wasn't the point. The thought of living through Campbell, through her father, appalled him. He had seen the scars from cigarette burns on Campbell's feet. Her father had done it to her, she explained. It was her father who had punished her with his red fingers the first time she menstruated. It was her father who kept her isolated and afraid, only gradually forming his ideas about how me might salvage something of her, drawing his plans like an astrologer his charts across great interplanetary gulfs and between the haunted stars. But her father no longer had a say in anything. When Varnas considered it in the right light, Campbell's wasting of her inheritance was its own form of revenge. By the time the cab returned him to his apartment on Park Avenue, the rain was torrential.

CHAPTER THREE

CAMPBELL GAVE THE CAB driver her address on Fifth Avenue. He
was a thin young man with watchful brown eyes, and he shivered
in the crosswind that agitated the wet gutters. He said something
about the grim weather in a low, hustling voice that struck her as
put on, yet no more than hers had been over drinks and caviar.
Could the young man tell she had been drinking? Under the black
canopy of the car, she applied lipstick, aware that it would be lost
in the rain between the curbside and her front door. Waiting for a
trolley to cross before them, Campbell asked the young man why
he didn't have any gloves to drive, and he explained that he had
given them to a derelict near Washington Square. At least when
the night's driving was done, unlike that man, he could afford
a room. Other guys, he said, would lose their frostbitten fingers
when the winter came for real. Campbell saw him watching her in
the mirror. She determined to keep her expression blank.

Campbell could not resist probing at the mind of the skinny,
young cab driver. She concentrated, testing at the limits of his
consciousness. She had practiced this telepathy with Charles
Varnas, guessing playing cards, copying images that he formed in
his mind and tried to conceal from her. Practicing with Varnas,
who would not lie to her, she could confirm her accuracy, or
her lack of it. She steadied her breathing in the chill. Already,

she perceived that her androgyny irritated him. His eyes told her that much, but Campbell went deeper yet, pushing into the lobes where his unconscious swarmed. She saw her fingernails parting the dank hair beneath his driving cap, opening the skin. Wiping blood from the bone, she smoothed over the skull, clean and white as a frozen planet, and passed into the webbing of the brain. There, she met a wall of grief and resentments: The cab driver's father had been shot in the face and died in the bloody slop of Belleau Wood. She purchased the date of June 6 at some cost to her posture, bending involuntarily toward the back of the driver's neck. She imagined her fingers pressing upon his contempt for her. He found her mouth attractive under its lipstick. He preferred it that way. He did not care for her masculine suit. His own class were too busy starving to simply play at being men, and only when they felt like it. Even his cabman's uniform connected him to his father's military drab. Such things as uniforms got you killed.

Campbell broke off, leaning back into her seat. She considered what she might say: that her father had really wanted a son, and he had been quite brutal in making her aware of this. That was the truth. She was faintly flushed, examining her dry fingers. Her desire to ask the cab driver if she was imagining all this was almost intolerable. She was also afraid that she was wrong. It would be humiliating to admit that this was all projection. As they approached her address with its vantage over Central Park, it seemed the young man eyed the opulent buildings like a sailor who has heard some islands are merely the backs of whales. Campbell paid him with a generous tip and stepped from the cab into the rain. The car pulled away.

On the sidewalk, she stood still, turned her face to the blackening sky, opened her mouth, and remained in that attitude until the cab drove away. The rain splashed upon her tongue. She thought of the distance that money set between people, and the impossibility of discourse between them when some were spectral, and some were flesh and blood. The survivors were those without bodies, like Varnas and her, she thought. Pursing her lips, she spat out the rainwater that had gathered in her mouth. Wiping with the back of her hand, the last red lipstick traces rubbed off. Campbell understood her toughness and that it might fail. That was all in the future, she thought, when Charles would understand his motives, at last. She was soaked through.

Her father had bequeathed this mansion to her. Inside, climbing the broad switching staircase to the fourth floor, the gravity of the empty rooms generated a low, hollow drone of absence, like the mourning engine of some phantom ship. It was, Campbell thought, quite reasonable that she should picture those spaces of her building filled with turbid water, dammed with drowned bodies, the old tenants. Opening the door to her home, she discovered that her suite of rooms was still warm. The fire had not yet perished in the grate. A few orange embers persisted in the ash. Above the white mantel, a smoked circular mirror with a golden ouroboros frame compassed her reflection between a pair of green lacquered skulls, trepanned for tall candles. Wax trailed and beaded their empty orbits of bone. Campbell lit the candles with cold, yet steady fingers.

The room had a high ceiling, and the candlelight was taken up by a chandelier like a glittering hive under its plaster ceiling rose. Turning back to the mantel, she checked her artifacts: a scuffed golf ball monogrammed R-O-C in emerald ink, and a postcard of Venice. Campbell scraped her wet hair back with her fingers and was cast in the mirror like a photograph of Lee Miller she had seen the year before, beautiful enough to emulate, she decided, with her blonde crop. It was only last year, she thought, when some hawk of avarice had come shrieking between the skyscrapers and snatched everything up—Campbell pictured her inheritance running out like golden sand in an hourglass. She thought of the financial district, so Promethean with its pecked-out liver. It would regrow, only to be pinched in that awful beak of ruin and return, again and again. Why should she be concerned about it? In the same way, the golden snakes of her hair would grow back. Lee

Miller's might, also. Campbell stirred the ashes in the fireplace and restored a small flame. She added some pages of *Vogue* and a small shovel of coal from the bucket beside the grate, before turning from the mantel to the expanse of her living room.

Her furniture was upholstered in ivory velvet, beige, and cream. The walls of her living room were a blue-green William Morris paper, and a collage of oriental rugs spread underfoot; a scattering of short Persian designs and a dominant Egyptian carpet where she conducted her communications. Her shadow exaggerated on the opposite wall and across her shelves of esoteric books. The smoke of the fireplace was comforting, and soon the rainwater began to lift from her clothes so that her lithe figure steamed, hot vapor against her calves. Some of Varnas' ejaculate was in her underwear, and some remained inside her. What did it matter if their moments had been anxious and furtive? That was the way of all things now, she thought. She wondered about Varnas and the superficial manner she had found to disguise herself as him, to reach him, as if imitating some lost part of his being could bring it back. Or was he disguising himself as, or in, her? Such were the dangerous provocations of being. Campbell had seen a ghost, but only once. It was not a white thing, nor a gray thing, but black as a domino.

Varnas lived north of Campbell, on Park Avenue. Now, the gin worked on him, so that the angles of his apartment disturbed him, set at the Expressionist angles of his mood. Somewhere inside the front door, his keys fell from his wet fingers. Nausea coiled in him. The vase of neglected lilies on the entry table gave off a sickly gas. In the living room, Varnas waved for the light switch and missed several times. He managed to remove the typewriter from its briefcase and placed it heavily on a side table. Locating a pair of scissors in a kitchen drawer, he concentrated upon cutting out the column on immortality from his stray page of newspaper, afraid that he might destroy it, but compelled to finish the task. Now, as rain whipped against the windowpanes, Varnas struggled to close the blue drapes without ripping them from their rods, clashing his hip against the leather flank of his Chesterfield. He thought of being with Campbell, her palms braced on the upholstery, yet there was no arousal in him that could survive the vertigo of the gin. Even when he remembered their scene in the descending elevator, he felt only the precipice of his enervation, the arcade of blackness beneath his consciousness. The darkness of his bedroom dragged at him, as he freed himself from his jacket and loosened his tie. His shirt was cold and soaked through.

At last, he fell back upon the bed and spread his arms. The backs of his hands slapped against the white linen. Light from the living room narrowed in the doorway. Some deranged version of himself desired to stay awake, but his eyes closed, heavy with the reddening glue of alcohol. For a moment, he was aware of the weight of his arms, stretching the muscles of his chest taut. He thought how terrible it must have been for Christ when God absented from his imagination, for Jesus to feel himself absolutely abandoned. How painful to believe it all lost and to be—for that moment—a man merely, suspended, and forsaken. It was to be taken to the brink, Varnas thought, then left trembling in the scope of your delusions, nailed to the wreckage of your knowledge, crying out, hopeless, only to be restored brightly from doubt once again, as if from a mad hoax. How Christ must have yearned to break his bloody wrists from the pins and ascend into the milky light he had been promised. Was any man's desire more mistaken, any violence more cruel? Varnas' mind protested with drunken vehemence. Should he ever claw from the gorgeous wasteland of alcohol, he might compose an ode to Aspirin. In the morning, he would be content with the chalky pills resting on his tongue, awaiting the tilt of a water glass. For now, he could not sleep, despite his fatigue. His mind raced. It raced toward Campbell, as though she were reeling him in.

Campbell, Charles Varnas thought, possessed grace in the way that a witch might possess a demon and duly render it afraid to desert her. Through his lens of gin, she was clearer to him than ever, enlarged. The insouciance he could feel during—but never after—a first drink, was precisely her nature at all times, and he envied it. Her diffidence protected her. He was different. It might develop slowly, even long after an evening had broken up, but he could become embittered, aggressive, and self-righteous of imagination, spoiling to make some correction to the world that he might not voice soberly. Whatever the first gifts of grain, they were soon lost to the chaff of his resentments. That, he recognized, was loneliness, some otherwise inexpressible melancholy that pressed upon him. He was, at last, a little afraid of himself, of the thoughtless shadow of his mind. Elegant, amoral, unburdened with contradiction—all that he failed to be—Campbell embodied. And she carried it with an uncanny ease. That's what a first drink is like, that quality of illumination, he thought, suffering the diminished returns of all the others. The original pleasure always lied to him about the next. His tongue was scarred with gin burns. He could feel it. Damn these spiritual thoughts—

If he could get up, he might crawl to the living room and find the telephone to call Campbell, but his flesh held him down, his blood leaden. His remorse would toil at him in the night. For now, it floated threateningly across the surface of his being. Varnas dreamed of something like a dark star. Too late, saw it plunging into the earth. Now, he slid into that coffin of his unconscious where Campbell slept, his image of her a waxwork warm from the cast. Her throat was lifted in dreaming, her mouth was open, as if to rainfall.

The newspaper clipping was beside Varnas' cheek when he awoke. His notebook was there, also. He did not remember writing anything. With these artifacts around him, the ghost of the gin protested in his eye sockets and pulled taut the thin flesh where his neck met the back of the skull. That was familiar to him. When drunk, some imperceptible tension prevented his head from sinking into the pillow, but being held just so, would turn his tendons into ropes of pain in the dark. Breathing slowly, he found that the newspaper cutting retained the smell of hot machinery, the vats of ink, the scent of a distant forest fire. He folded it inside his notebook of poems. Aloud, he asked it, "What do you want?" and pushed it lower, over the sandy brocade of his coverlet. He had dreamed of the Adversary, lying dead on the dune. Yet, there was no face, only a disembodied presence.

CHAPTER FOUR

THAT MORNING, FOLLOWING THE communion of Aspirin that Varnas had longed for, he and Campbell took their breakfast at Katz's. Vapor haunted the subway, and the sidewalk was glassy from the night's deluge. The streets were busy under the dripping awnings. The glare of sunlight spread across the deli's red brick and poured in through the windows, imposing pedestrian shadows across the walls and the ceiling. Inside, they took their tickets and placed their orders. Campbell insisted on paying, and Varnas teased her about letting him off her leash, one day. She told him simply that she liked to pay, and *That's All!* As the sign above the window said. He laughed, and acquiesced. The air was pungent and heavy. Varnas draped his herringbone coat over the back of his chair. He had dressed casually in a cream shirt with a pocket, and no tie. He studied the bluish shadows beneath Campbell's green eyes as she shrugged off her beige raincoat. The tips of her shoulders gleamed beneath a white silk blouse and man's under-shirt. Her black tie dangled, undone, animated by her breathing. Even through the pall of his hangover, and in her androgynous attitude, still he found her mesmerizing. She possessed an almost preternatural quality of adapting to her surroundings, he thought, in the way that certain seahorses shift their color. She was a strange, modern chameleon. He watched her as she appraised the counter, the bearded men with their strong coffee, payot curling under dark hats. Varnas wondered how it must be to live inside such an ortho-doxy of spirit. Did they suffer more, or less, or merely differently? Campbell regarded a Modigliani woman in a brown trench coat holding forth at the counter; a skinny man in a baggy gray suit, holding a brown paper sack and a homburg hat under one arm, chewing on a dead cigarette; and the entrance of a youthful police-man with his cap tilted back, beaming relief to get a break from his beat. She noticed them as if preparing for a series of potential dangers. It was, Varnas thought, her glamorous paranoia, and he supposed that he shared in it. He said, "How did you sleep?"

"Alone." Lifting her coffee cup, but without drinking, she announced, "I was thinking about your ghost."

"Yes?"

"We both know who it is."

"We do?"

Campbell let silence hang between them for several seconds, her eyes gleaming, before she lifted an accent from a raven-haired woman at the next table. "Such a putz, he is." And yet, she was astonished. Varnas really didn't know who, or what haunted him. Five years, she thought. "Still, I've decided that you—that we— shouldn't go to a seance." That was all she intended to say. Just enough to sound him out. Even that, she conceded, was reckless, but she was in a good and reckless mood.

"Oh, why not?"

She diverted. "I miss Italy, don't you? Venice, mostly, I suppose. Clouds reflecting in the surface of the canals. Would you go back to Europe if I procured us a pair of tickets?"

"God, I don't know." He rubbed his eyes with the palm of his hand. "I mean, I would, I suppose. But the dollar isn't worth a dime." He was aware that this was an excuse, but it was not without merit. It got him off the hook.

Campbell grinned. "I just wanted to know that you might. One day, we might need to make an escape."

"I have good memories of Venice, sure," he said. "Paris, most definitely. And Florence was nice."

She crooned, "Florence—*Caravaggio*—" Beneath the table, her feet in polished black loafers tested his shins, before settling softly upon his shoes.

Varnas could not know then that he was being both provoked and tamed, lured into her fatal luminescence. "I could barely drag you away from *Medusa*," he recalled. "But another month or two on a ship, Campbell? Could you even stand it? I do remember something of that," he smiled. Varnas surrendered to her nostalgia. He tried to recall the Caravaggio that had impressed him the most, but something prevented it. He was drinking too much, and it was erasing his memories, he thought. And yet, it was impossible to imagine the agonies of exposure he would suffer without its glassy armor. The painting would come back to him, in time. Who could say when any memory might return? Each had a life of its own.

"Oh, and do you remember what I said about her—about *Medusa*?" Campbell wiped pastrami grease from her lips with a white napkin.

"Christ, you're lovely."

"Not that."

Varnas acquiesced. "You said that Medusa had petrified a great many men who looked at her, perhaps as many as a baseball stadium holds, before that sly Perseus decapitated her with his sword."

"Come on. That's the easy part. Everyone knows that."

"All right." He readied himself, shifting in his seat and pushing strands of peroxided hair from his eyes. He prepared to enter her perspective, like a conjoined twin. "You want it verbatim. All right. It's scored into the gramophone of my skull. You said, the truth is that the man is petrified of the woman because her interior is unknowable and serpentine to him. The inside of Perseus' shield was polished until it had the quality of a fine mirror. And here, you insisted that the shield or the mirror became an artificial lens: the lens of the eye of Culture. Perseus could not look at Medusa, directly. Man never looks at woman, directly. Perseus used his polished shield of Culture to stalk her through the ashen statues and bloody colonnades of her island. Watching her in the frame and confines of that reflection, he regarded her voluptuous head of serpents, and struck it from her neck."

"That's not bad, is it?" Campbell said.

"No, it's good. You're very clever. And I asked you, who gave Perseus the shield? And you said, it was a woman, of course. And so, then you said—"

"—Never feel pity for a woman."

"Do you really want to go back, Campbell?" If he had glanced at her, he would have noticed her smirk. He continued before she could answer. "I had terrible dreams last night, do you know? Right now, I can only imagine that going back, returning, whatever it should be called, would be dangerous."

"Dangerous?"

"Not physically—Can we change the subject?"

"Of course. What would you prefer? But if you're trying to avoid talking about sex and death, give it up. One is always talking about sex and death, particularly when one tries to avoid the subjects. Freud would tell you."

"Campbell, can you envision a man who suspects he might be immortal, but who lacks the courage to test the proposition? He has certain information. But he won't throw himself from a precipice or a tall building, or drink poison, or wilt into the path of a taxi or a subway car to prove it. Can you imagine a man who waits, patiently, watching as everything around him gently perishes? Only, you see, his memory is quite short—too short to remind him of the evidence of his endless being." Like a poem that no one has read, he thought. Charles Varnas lifted his knife, and saw Campbell, now reflected in the blade, her short hair, green eyes, and maddening lips. "Sometimes, of late, I feel like that."

"You should be careful," she said.

"What?"

"With thoughts like that."

Varnas spoke gently. "That was stupid of me. Forgive me. I didn't mean the bit about the tall building, really."

"Be careful with time, Charles, that's all. You can be a genuine bloody brute. Do you know that?"

After they had eaten, they put on their coats and walked in silence for several city blocks. A pall had draped itself over them. Varnas caught something of their reflection in the white-washed glass of an abandoned storefront, two blond and dissolute phantoms. The scar beside his right eye itched. Campbell seemed to weep silently, without tears, even. Only the way she would pull her pale chin toward her throat, and the intermittent shrug of her shoulders, the way her lips parted as if to gasp at the air betrayed her. Then, she would lift her face brightly, as if she had cupped her hands full of freezing water and tossed it against her cheeks. They drifted to Tomkins Square where the elms were golden and sounded like a subtle language in the breeze. Campbell kicked through the fallen leaves. Across the park, men slept on the grass, sprawled in ragged groups like fresh corpses that had faced a firing squad.

"I'm sorry," Varnas said, turning slightly away from her in shame.

"It's all right. It's almost a year, but not quite. Don't you dare pity me. I can do that myself. Sometimes, when I'm in my right mind, I don't care, because I remember how bad things were. I'm glad he is gone." She collapsed toward him and kissed the edge of his mouth. A single frame of her father's existence flickered beneath her awareness, for this is how she had kissed him the last time, one last deceit before they had tried to run from him.

Varnas held her then and wondered if wounding her with his talk of suicide had been his careless, unconscious way of arranging this moment, of testing the terrible, tender gravity between them.

CHAPTER FIVE

CAMPBELL'S FATHER, RAFFERTY ORAN Campbell, was fifty years old at the time of his death, and she twenty-nine, born on the shining edge of the coin toss century. What had distinguished her father was not his retired swimmer's build, nor the brooding glamor of the man in his domino-dark suits, not his peat-black hair, not the wild grief muscle that announced his memories pulling at his brow like a fishhook, nor the swift and substantial fortune he had gathered. He had gone with a widower's ironic grace through the whispering lounges of the city, with that latent, unspeakable *thing*—all of the unspeakable *things*—of which he was suspected. What distinguished Campbell's father, at least in his daughter's eyes, was his timing—the side of Black Thursday he had chosen to plummet from the parapet of the Bankers Trust Company Building. It was another kind of loss that had worn him out. And one thing remained true that had been so all of his life—it was better to exit at the right moment than to be discovered, to be revealed in his subtle malevolence, to be unmasked forever. His funeral was private, unattended even by his daughter or Charles Varnas.

Rafferty Oran Campbell was not on the side of the ledger that would later be called neurotic, neurasthenic, or despairing, and whose flesh fell with their fortunes into the well-stocked streets of ruin. It seemed to his daughter that some dignified prescience had kept him from the list of those designated as 'suicides' or 'jumpers' in the wake of the Crash—

That woman Borowski of whom she had read in the *Times,* falling forty stories last November—Or, the one whose name was lost to her, but who had poisoned himself three weeks after that— That man Cutler dropping five hundred feet onto the canopy of a parked car—And this was not to speak of the ones dragged out of the rippling gas of kitchen ovens, the one who set himself on fire that December of Twenty-nine and killed his wife also, and not to mention all the bullets to broke brains—

They all made the papers, she recalled. Her father's death was, quite simply, seven days too early for such an interpretation, on the other side of that mocking solstice of money, that wicked equinox of wealth. On that side of the Crash, it was still possible to see such a fall from a tall building in the Financial District as a tragic accident.

Yet, Rafferty Oran Campbell had been contemplating his exit for some time. It was one of his instincts, to know when to exit, and if and when to return. His sense that the Crash was coming merely loaned it an urgency. He had possessed his own pain. Egoist that he was, he could not stand to be misunderstood. He could not stomach the notion of false motives being attributed to his end by the public, even as he kept his true motives carefully concealed. He would have to go before the Crash or be forever compromised. His enemies would not be allowed to think of him as a pathetic casualty of that October 24th, 1929. More importantly, neither would his daughter. She would know precisely what darkness had driven him. And he could disappear into it for as long as he desired. They believed that they had cornered and defeated him, but he had merely slipped into the wings, biding his time, forcing his daughter to mourn, even against her hatred of him. And they would always suspect and fear his return. It was inevitable. If they found any peace, it would yield nothing more than a sense of sleeping beneath a guillotine. Thus, he hoped to destroy her, and to destroy Charles Varnas.

Now, his daughter sat on the living room floor of her Fifth Avenue suite, in the grand building that she had inherited from him, dressed in black, cross-legged on her wide Egyptian rug. She had spooned a silver pentagram of fireplace ash from a saucer over the colorful weave. As she bent over the design, her Isis pendant swung from the collar of her shirt. Campbell felt like a strange bird, her body contested by opposed wings that might tear her apart—her father's sly and furious Miltonian tradition and the instinct she possessed for the muddy sand and dreaming hollows of the Nile. Eclectic and modern as she was, Campbell experienced herself like a tattered seam between them, some icy light breaking through her stitches.

Campbell's pentagram was arrayed at its cardinal points with burning candles in short brass cups. Beyond this occult perimeter, she had pulled all the heavy curtains closed, and observed the precaution of covering the mirror above the mantle with her black silk headscarf. The candles that protruded from the green lacquered skulls were lit, also. A block of kyphi incense also burned there on the mantel, spilling rosemary and pine-scented smoke from the myrrh and mastic. In the angles of her lap was a chromed flask of old Irish whiskey, most of which she had finished while laying out her ceremony. Close to her left knee was a single tarot card she had drawn from her deck and set face down upon the carpet. There was a faint cramp behind her right knee, and the drink had left her with a foul thirst and pinched her brow with the early thorns of a hangover. Had she been able to regard herself in the covered mirror, she might have caught something of her father's pained aspect in her face, the intimation of pleading in the ivory skin above her green eyes. Time crawled. The darkness and the tarot card awaited their turn. Campbell sucked on the whiskey once more, letting the alcohol sit on her tongue where it burned as though it might dissolve her. She cast the empty flask aside and it vanished without a sound into the soft shroud of the room, as though someone had caught it. At last, in the fluttering light of her ritual, Campbell inhaled and exhaled slowly, three times. She flipped the card over. The image did not surprise her. Unconsciously, she had been waiting for it—The Devil—

She saw him then—on the ledge below the pyramid that formed the final seven stories before the peak of the Bankers Trust Company Building—The Devil made for high places, and she was within him, inside him, occupying him like a hermit crab a foreign shell—and his handsome ghost was present in her skin, a second pale pulse echoing at her wrist, a subtle animation of the red gloss of her lips—the last words he spoke, freighted with infinite disappointment, before flexing his ankles, and leaning from the ledge—*I can't see the stars*—Campbell fell with him into that sinister, inviting column of emptiness between the tall buildings. She felt it all. At the last moment, he had given a small kick with his toes like a swimmer on his mark, a diver on his board. The freezing air that cornered Nassau and Wall Street blasted her face, stripping her senses with the violence of a breath that had the hunger of four billion years behind it. She wanted to scream, but because her father—in whom she fell—did not, she could not. Presently, in that unity, she experienced his relaxation, and in a tall window she caught a glimpse of a man in a black suit with his arms outstretched, exhibiting his form, hanging defiantly in space, five hundred feet above the ground—Now, the cold air held him, upside-down, like the crucified Saint Peter. Something about this image—was it a flicker of Caravaggio or a reflection in a lagoon that took her back to some morning with Charles Varnas?—something permitted her an infinitesimal distance from him. It was enough of a distance to allow some appraisal of the man careening through emptiness. Poor, queer Daddy, she thought, without sentimentality—In 1901, his wife Lilith, the mother Campbell had never known, drowned. Her mother had slipped from the deck of their yacht off the beaches of East Hampton and vanished under feathered waves of brine forever. Everyone believed that Rafferty Oran

Campbell had murdered his wife, of course. Yes, he had wanted
a son. As he fell, Campbell searched beneath the calm of his skin,
inside the cool resignation of his psyche for some image of her
mother, but none came. Lilith—Lilith—her mother with feet like
a bird's—No, she had faded in the twenty-eight years they lived
without her, and there had never been enough of her, never sufficient presence for Campbell to contact her, even here. Suddenly,
the space collapsed, and she was within her falling father again,
inside her Devil, streaming toward the street like a black ribbon
tied to a coin. There, she thought, there was an image of damna-
tion. And she wondered if it was her thought, or her father's.

Campbell remembered. She was a child, alone on a windswept
beach of gray pebbles that hurt her small feet when she tried to
walk upon them. Someone had carried her along the shore to
where a plaid blanket had been unfolded and weighted down with
a picnic basket. Of that presence that bore her across the cruel
stones, she recalled merely the dark skin of the fingers, holding her
beneath her armpits, setting her down, undoing the leather strap
from the shining buckles of the hamper, and pointing across the
choppy water to a white sail like paper curling in steam. It was her
father's boat, listing in the fog. They seemed to be a man's fingers.
Now, she was unsure. She wondered how much of it was real.
What explained her ambivalence toward him, and his reckless,
unrelenting cruelty? How did one love under a strap, under so
many insults to skin and self? When he had tortured her, whence
this weird pity? Was it, in the end, some common grief? How
much of his evil was in her? How should one live with the knowledge that one's father is the Devil? It was good that Charles could
not recall everything that had happened. It protected him. It was
not hers to tell, for she had not been with him. And it was impossible to imagine. She understood that there were ways in which she
was Charles' devil. It was in the killing that he advocated for her.

Charles Varnas had been unable to sleep. He found himself outside the Campbell mansion on Fifth Avenue, staring up at her lightless windows. It took all of his presence not to cry out to her. He had the feeling that perhaps he had slept very briefly. Vaguely, he recalled that he had dreamt that he was falling and had lunged, gasping into wakefulness. He remembered the way his body snapped like a folded belt. He was ecstatic—Abruptly, Campbell's curtains were flung back, and light blazed from inside her suite above the empty floors below. The French doors to her small balcony opened, and he watched her come out backwards into the night, as if dragging a corpse. It was one of her oriental carpets, the wide Egyptian rug. Varnas watched as she struggled to haul it half over the balustrade, then slapped it several times with her open hand, releasing a pallid cloud of backlit dust. What was she doing at this time of night? Campbell did not see him, far below on the sidewalk.

Campbell took the dusted carpet back inside, and set it in place, kicking the corners flat. The pentagram was erased. She had extinguished all of the candles and set the brass cups on a shelf of her bookcase. Exhausted, she went along the short hallway, past the white tiled bathroom to her bedroom. She checked the safe that was concealed inside her bedside table, rotating the bevel, and unlatching the heavy handle. What was left inside was all that remained of the cash in her father's estate, belted bricks of paper. Somehow, in its stark and shadowed sarcophagus, the money had seemed infinite. Yet, it had diminished with the months of depression and her laissez-faire disinterest in its future. How long it would take to burn through it, she was not certain. Campbell possessed no natural caution, nor any sense of thrift. She could not imagine herself needing to chase money, as others did. Some dark providence observed her and dispensed its luck with gratuity. Something would happen, she felt, to render the money unimportant again. She resolved to remain unconcerned.

CHAPTER SIX

KHALED'S PLACE IN EZBEKIYA—THAT night, five years ago, retreating from the place where he had killed, Charles Varnas folded himself into a scalloped cane chair, comfortable as a bed of reeds, pulling the blue silk drape from its high back onto his shoulders in the monarchy of his drunkenness. He dropped his blanched linen jacket onto the dirty floor and smiled to himself. The cabaret was finished for the night, yet there were still some stubborn, insomniac patrons—mostly Europeans and Americans—weaving through the fog of cigarettes with glimmering cocktail glasses. With his index finger, he hooked a strand of dark hair from his right eye, felt the heavy sweat, and then—with something like nostalgia—traced the hawthorn scar that ran horizontally from the corner of his eye to his hairline level with his ear. Before him, someone had left an open box of England's Glory matches on the white metal table. The ashtray overflowed.

Varnas turned his attention to the red-painted stage with its two tin can footlights. The stage was now empty, except for a gramophone on a folding card table, and a teetering stack of records. The gramophone issued an asthmatic rendition of Isham Jones' "Kismet" that shrugged against his nerves like a cat wearing a collar of wicked pins, but it set the sole of his shoe tapping brightly against the tile floor. The stage had a microphone for singing. As

Varnas saw it, it was not inconceivable that the room belonged at the end of the last pier in the world, hanging over an abyss of black water, not this white-palmed square in the desert. In the daylight, the square was fringed with French gardens, booksellers, European-style hotel façades, and a new department store, among its labyrinthine alleys. That night, it was the illumination of the department store—Tiring's, with its glowing cupola and crystal globe held up by four casts of Atlas facing the winds—that had been his star to navigate by.

Now, like a bad dream, a small monkey on a leash capered at the end of the bar. It seemed to Varnas that every person inside Khaled's Place was emaciated. When a woman laughed, it was like hearing a gunshot. Khaled prowled behind the bar. He reminded Varnas of a skeletal Douglas Fairbanks, dressed in the tuxedo of an exhumed corpse, swatting absently at flies with his blue striped towel. There were only seven tables and five chairs, beside the one he occupied. An Egyptian read an old copy of the *Telegraph* at one of the tables. It was as if the man had forgotten where he was, Varnas thought. Several of the tourists at Khaled's had set themselves at the long counter and sipped from tiny metal coffee cups and an irregular collection of thick glassware. They slouched in the way drunks will when they're listening intently to things they will forget in the morning. And Charles Varnas felt that he was struggling already to recall anything. He had some fragmentary knowledge that he was to rendezvous with someone here. He was in shock. There was no doubt about that. Something had come down between him and the murder of the Adversary.

The music from the gramophone swooped and jittered, and a young man in a battered fez came to the place where Varnas sat. Varnas found it hard to concentrate on the man's face. On a tin tray, he bore a glass of gin set upon a folded sheet of ivory notepaper. The young man spoke with a thick accent. "She said you would need this, Mr. Varnas," he said, and inclined his head discretely toward a woman who had been seated beneath a skinny indoor palm, but who had risen now, and was approaching Varnas' table. The young man retreated briskly, his tray at his side. Varnas shook the note open. It said, simply, "Well done."

Closer now, the woman was as emaciated as every other person there. She wore her hair beneath a black silk scarf. All of her clothes, the trousers, the silk blouse, were black. When she was six feet away, with her left hand she began dragging a metal chair behind her as though it were something she had killed. She possessed an ominous nonchalance, he thought. Something of the confusion that hung on him from the killing lifted. It was Campbell. Varnas was relieved. They had been careful. No one knew them. No one paid them any attention. Campbell swiveled the chair and seated herself close to him. The grating of the chair as she approached had been such that he had not noticed the drink in her other hand, something brown that she sipped, crossing her thin legs so that her knee disturbed the table. It was obvious that Campbell was quite drunk, as detached from her surroundings as he was. She was, he thought, forcing herself to be remote, seeking some dispassionate attitude to inhabit.

Varnas snatched his glass and lifted it, thanking her for the gin. He glanced at the stage and asked Campbell if he had missed anything. In her cool voice, she explained that the cabaret singer had not shown up that evening, so Khaled himself had climbed onto the stage and read a poem in English. The microphone had shrieked terribly from his being too close, or too far away, or because of his metal front tooth, she wasn't sure. The poem she had found almost incomprehensible in the Egyptian's accent and lost rhythm—it was something by Shelley. He was sorry to have missed it.

They were silent for a moment.

Varnas wondered if the tremors he felt were visible to her. Something in his blood, or in the grotesqueries of the bar, reminded him of his fading horror, one last intimation of guilt in his nerves. He wondered what part she played in the coming down of the screens between himself and the act. No, he thought, not her.

"You really did it," Campbell said. She managed to smile in her aloof manner, and with great effort said, "Happy birthday."

Varnas studied her as he tasted the gin. She had the look of someone who had been crying an hour ago, and whose green eyes were bloodshot and slow to recover. Without lipstick, her mouth was pale and dry. She was still beautiful for all that.

"We'll pay for it," he said.

"Yes." She hesitated, emptied her glass in one movement and brightened automatically. Campbell raised her hand and snapped her fingers in the smoke. "But not tonight."

The young man in the fez brought more drinks. Varnas lit a match from the abandoned box on the table and started a cigarette. After dragging on the smoke, he dropped Campbell's note onto the heaped ashtray and burned it—

Then, they were at Shepheard's Hotel. It seemed, like their previous hotel in Venice, to have been constructed around an opulent part of the city, interrupted by ancient palm trees and potent columns of stone, a dome with striped oriental windows, urns of bladed foliage, lotus, and papyrus leaves. The facade was distinctly colonial with its neo-classical balustrades and balconies, wicker chairs and cane tables, and the metal café pavilions which, like an aviary, occupied the pavement. He retained the dim sense of seeing two nudes holding electric light bulbs, and for a moment considered that they might have been real, not sculpture. Varnas was pleased to discover that the room next to theirs was silent, even when he stood close to the smooth white wall, putting his ear against it. For some time, he and Campbell lay beside one another on the bed, above the bronze coverlet, and he knocked his knuckle gently and repeatedly against the headboard. At last, she took his hand. It was trembling. But everything would be all right, he said. She turned his palm up and traced the lines.

"Yes, this hand is the same unchanged hand," she said, seeking to reassure him. "It is just as it has always been. There's the heart line. That's where you'll find me, deep in that warm trench of skin." She smiled in the lamplight. "Like a splinter you can't get at. It can't be changed."

"There could never be anyone else, Campbell."

She looked into his eyes. "You love me, despite everything?"

"I love you, Campbell."

Turning her attention back to his palm, she said, "Here is the life line, still strange in the way it divides, as if you have two lives. No wonder you're so paranoid, dear Charles."

"You don't think you have some responsibility for that?"

"Look how the sun line intersects with it—"

"So what?"

"Fame or infamy, that's a damned strong line you have, for one or the other. Let's celebrate. I'll buzz for some champagne."

Campbell had procured some peroxide, and he found it in the tiled bathroom. That evening was the last time she, or anyone else, would see his natural hair color. It took a long time to drunkenly bleach out the raven shade. He recalled that his eyelids were burning and red from the chemicals, and he felt estranged from everything. They had made love and he had collapsed, reckless and ashamed into her bones, the knife gleam of her pelvis in the Egyptian moonlight. He had only a distant sense of his own evil, but it was real, and this had met a profound denial. As soon as it had happened, a blankness had assumed the scene. Now, Varnas shivered in the dog sleep that came to him after drinking. His flesh sensed the hour, and that—with three more remaining until dawn—he would not sleep again. An abstract remorse set him flinching in the white sheets, whimpering, and wanting to die. He did not know how long they could stay in Egypt. Yet, he dreaded the crossing back to New York.

CHAPTER SEVEN

"ARE WE HAPPY, CHARLES?" This Campbell asked him on the morning after that deluge when she had summoned the fallen shade of her father, and unbeknownst, Varnas had stood below her window in the bleak and pelted street. Now the sun was shining, hard and hieroglyphic in the pale sky.

"Of course. I believe so," he said.

She snaked her arm tighter into the tweed crook of his elbow as they walked. "But—" The word hung over several yards of their circuit of Central Park before she could finish the thought. "Were we, you know, happier before?"

"No."

"That's right, isn't it?"

Varnas watched the sheep on the meadow. It was as though some muddy acreage of England had been grafted there, between the tall buildings and taxi cabs, the stubborn grass vivid and the animals numinous in the sunlight. "Let's go and see them." As they walked among the sheep and touched their fleeces, Varnas lifted his fingers to his face to breathe in the thick scent of lanolin. It awakened something in him, an association. At that moment, he wanted more than anything else to tell her about a time in his childhood.

The boy that he had been in 1912 was in his school classroom, close to the back of the room because of the order of his surname. The lidded desks were in stark rows, the boys having etched each interior obscenely with their compass points, and sharpened pencils. Young Varnas did not mind being at the back. Disappearing appealed to him. He was seated upon a hard wooden chair, dressed in the gray uniform that seemed to him to have been chosen to match the dour quality of the weather that had settled over that part of Oxfordshire. His family might have brought it from the North, he thought, and felt pleased with himself. At the front of the class, Mr. Hulme stood before a broad blackboard, a fine white dust of chalk on his robes, one fist clenched, the other hand open, to support a worn, almost spineless Bible. Hulme, crow-haired, soot-eyed, and hard as an iron lamppost, had been reading from Genesis 11, watching between verses to be certain that the boys were paying attention to his sermon. His mouth was firm and serious as he elaborated and improvised upon the Tower of Babel. Charles Varnas liked Mr. Hulme, because his family had also come down from the North; there remained a trace of a Lancashire accent in his teaching voice. Pinned to the wall was a reproduction of Bruegel's painting of the Tower, reminiscent of a cracked hive with something desperate and fleshy exposed, vast aorta and vessels screeching under a limpid gray-blue sky cut with gathering clouds. Hulme was telling the boys about why there are different races, different tongues, the great majority of which, even if they knew a little French, or Latin, they would never see on paper, nor hear in their various airs, "so capacious," he said, "is the canopy of the world." His accent drew out the last word. The other two dozen boys in the room listened passively to the master, his strong charismatic voice. Hulme turned to his own imitation of the Tower—a stack of books at the edge of his desk. "But, look," he demanded "what the people have done with their imagination!" He began dismantling the Tower and putting the books in disparate places, declaiming, "Thus, thus, thus!" He tossed several books at the polished oak floor where they slid between the feet of his class. Pages broke from the spines of some of the older books and flapped in the breeze of an open window.

The story seemed one of the cruelest Charles Varnas had heard yet—this God who was against imagination, of all things, and punished you for it. Was God jealous of Varnas' own quiet creations? Knowing the full depth of the danger, he raised his hand to speak, to offer his disappointed dissent. Something in him rebelled against this puerile God, and he would not be silent. Indignant, his hand trembled in the air, as though it were made of paper. Was it, then, dangerous to write his poems? Suddenly, his throat closed, and it became difficult to breathe. Glancing in panic to the window with its gray mullion and black lead, he glimpsed the white sheep on the green angle of ground outside. Imagining his fingers against their fleece, the deep scent of lanolin, the brightness of the dewy grass released him. Slowly, he lowered his hand. It was a motion as involuntary, as unconscious as the one that first raised his agitated finger through the haze of chalk dust to poke God in his eye. He felt weak. While Hulme was talking, the door to the classroom opened. Later, he would think that if his hand been raised still, his finger lifted accusingly, then Hulme might have seen him at the back of the class and engaged him in conversation before the door opened, and things might have been different—

Mr. Knight, the headmaster, entered and scanned the room with his dishwater eyes, and one fey loll of his white-haired skull on his white neck found Varnas in his seat. The master's robes, Varnas thought, made him look like a gigantic bat. Hulme had ceased talking the moment that Knight stepped across the thin brass threshold onto the wooden classroom floor. "Might I have Varnas?" Knight said.

Varnas rose quietly and obediently and walked between the desks to the front of the room, following Knight—who said nothing else—out into the corridor.

Knight led the way, glancing back over his shoulder and smiling kindly. "You don't need that simple class, Charles. Though Mr. Hulme is a good man, it's beneath you." They passed through a set of double doors. Only when the hinges had pinched the doors closed behind them had Charles understood that they were walking in the direction of Knight's study. "Consider yourself rescued, young man."

Varnas thrilled in silence for a moment, liberated from that unimaginative, resentful God of Genesis, and then composed himself. "Thank you, Sir."

They continued along the corridor with the headmaster explaining. "Charles, the most difficult thing to believe in is the truth. Because the truth may have become unfashionable, or it may be absurd. Ask Kierkegaard if you don't believe me. It can be lonely." The headmaster seemed to sense Charles' confusion. "Look. We have something better for you. Henceforth, you will not attend Mr. Hulme's class, but will have tea with me in my study, instead. We will talk, but not as master and pupil, exactly. How does that sound?" Presently, Knight opened his study door and ushered the boy Varnas inside. "I hear you've been writing some very interesting poems, Charles. It's very important that— should you wish to be a poet—"

The earnest boy interrupted. "I do!"

"Then you must go directly to the divine matter, the best stuff, as you might have it. That's what we'll discuss. What do you think of that?"

"I'd like that. I want to be a poet." Charles went to the window and saw the sheep again.

"Good." Knight pushed and angled a chair close enough to his desk for Charles to sit, take tea, and see the pages of various books at the same time. "So," Knight continued, "this is where I live. In the daylight, at least," Knight poured milk into gold-rimmed cups from a small porcelain jug. "You like tea, I presume, as any young Englishman does." He smiled.

Varnas nodded. He sat at the desk and glanced at the heavy bookcases with their hundreds of volumes. It was strange and overwhelming.

"It was Mr. Hulme who told me about your poems. He told me that he's never seen so much promise in a boy, and barely twelve years of age. Imagine that."

"They're not my best, Sir...the ones he has from class."

"I'm certain of that. But promise is promise. Speaking of which, can you promise that our talks are kept strictly private, between us only?"

"I promise." The boy sipped his tea. He studied the crucifix that hung from a nail on the wall behind the schoolmaster's chair.

Knight took in the boy's recognition. "Yes, unfashionable," he smirked. "I shall read something to you." Smiling, he picked a compact leather notebook from his desk, and turned the pages toward a thin black ribbon he had used to keep his place. "You see, I have an old poet friend named Bridges," Knight explained. "He lives at Boars Hill, which is a good place for poets, with slopes, and hedgerows, and birdsong. Bridges is declining now, and his lungs are bad. He's quite solitary. But you see, Charles, he confided this poem to me." The headmaster tapped his notebook with his finger. "It's not one of his own, though. Bridges was friends with a man named Hopkins who became a Jesuit. Hopkins was quite long deceased when I came to know Bridges. But the poem struck me, powerfully. The next time I visited Bridges, when he would absent himself briefly from his study, I would copy it down in fugitive pieces. He would return from his coughing and offer me sherry. He never knew I was copying the poem down." Knight grinned and began to read from his notebook.

I caught this morning morning's minion, king-
dom of daylight's dauphin, dapple-dawn-drawn Falcon, in his riding
Of the rolling level underneath him steady air, and striding
High there, how he rung upon the rein of a wimpling wing

In his ecstasy! then off, off forth on swing,
  As a skate's heel sweeps smooth on a bow-bend: the hurl and gliding
  Rebuffed the big wind. My heart in hiding
Stirred for a bird,—the achieve of, the mastery of the thing!

Brute beauty and valour and act, oh, air, pride, plume, here
  Buckle! AND the fire that breaks from thee then, a billion
Times told lovelier, more dangerous, O my chevalier!

The schoolmaster broke off, lowered the book slightly as
asked, "Do you know what a 'chevalier' is?"

Charles Varnas, intoxicated, singular, the one boy selected to
hear all of this, to be so initiated, to know *something better*, shook
his head in happy confusion.

"It means 'knight'!" The headmaster tapped his own chest
with his fingers.

"Ah!" Charles said.

Knight laughed. Now, in his element, he inclined the notebook
once more, searching with his dishwater eyes, and continued:

No wonder of it: sheer plod makes plough down sillion
Shine, and blue-bleak embers, ah my dear,

  Fall, gall themselves, and gash gold-vermilion.

When he finished, Knight saw that the child was staring at
the book in amazement. "Isn't that good? That's what I mean,
Charles! And this poem that you heard, and almost no others have,
was dedicated to Christ. Do you understand it?"

"I didn't understand all of the words, but I heard and felt
what they meant." Charles Varnas was grinning, as though he
had discovered a treasure, even as he slurped his tea. He was not
embarrassed, and Knight wanted no shame in him. That, he could
tell. "I would say it was the best poem I've ever heard, Sir."

"The poet's full name was Gerard Manley Hopkins, a most
unfashionable believer, and a sometime schoolteacher. The title is
'The Windhover.' Now listen, this poem has not been published, but
we have it here, Charles, you and I. It is a secret between us. There

were other poems, once in Hopkins' hand, now in mine, here. What should one say about a stolen poem when it is God's poem?"

"I'll never forget it," Varnas said.

"It's an *immortal* poem," Knight said, "even if might never be published, and remain forever in the shadows." His voice was pleasant and musical. "Indeed, it may well remember us, more than *we* remember *it*. It will outlive us both, and all of this. That's the beauty of poems, isn't it?" He waved toward the window with the back of his hand. "For the present, let us appreciate our time here, now, together."

Charles Varnas was happy—

If Charles Varnas could have told this story to Campbell as they were that morning in Central Park, close to the sheep meadow, he would have told her about the crash of those teacups upon the wooden floor, when that thing happened, and happened every week for months that would twist the boy into shame and silence. It did not happen on the first occasion he was removed from Mr. Hulme's class, or the second. But it happened from that point onward, into painstaking desolation and slow crucifixion. The spring of his pencil poems stilled, frozen under the ever-colder gleam of Knight's eye, the gestures of his skin over the boy and the desk. Finally, the suffering stopped when Knight fell from his hunting horse after a fox. Varnas imagined a kestrel riding its hang over the dogslick stirrup, the slimed whip and the lickspittle hounds coming to the unconscious man. How could Christ have witnessed it all, and failed to intervene? Or even Mr. Hulme, who must have known or suspected. This, the boy had asked himself, until he was too old for Christ. Yet, Charles Varnas had kept his promise, even as it seemed an absurd, cruel silence to hold. It was the first time that he had considered mortality in its meanness, menace, and meaning. He thought about silence now, the silence of forgetting.

PART TWO

I can give not what men call love,
But wilt thou accept not
The worship the heart lifts above
And the Heavens reject not,—
The desire of the moth for the star,
Of the night for the morrow,
The devotion to something afar
From the sphere of our sorrow?

—Percy Bysshe Shelley, from "To —"

CHAPTER EIGHT

"Sometimes," Campbell said, "I think that I'm being followed by some wretched little Egyptian detective." And yet, the relentless specter her anxiety had constructed was not wretched at all, but quite reminiscent of Rudolph Valentino, and he followed beautiful and brooding in pinstripe, and in dark glasses with striking oval eyes underneath, the luminescent whites, smoked pupils and shadows exaggerated by his narrowed lids. Her imaginary detective's hair was sleek and black as a hearse. His lips, she considered, possessed the clear definition of ancient statuary. Yet, for all that, she suspected that he was slight of build, light-boned, furtive enough to go tapering into crowds. The suggestion of his presence haunted her and left her ambivalent. She deserved it, did she not? Would she like to see him, and be certain?

Campbell and Varnas had emerged from Central Park, and she had insisted that he let her buy another lunch at the Cloud Club, their own Tower of Babel. She felt there was nothing else to do and was listless and louche in the park because her flesh was charged and sparking for gin. Had Prohibition made it more acute? She did not know or care. Yet, she determined that she had been a good sport when Varnas had needed her to be, trailing her fingers through the greasy fleece of several sheep, and humoring him as he stared at something unknowable, something not quite present.

At last, intuiting that the reverie which captured him was fading away—or did he shove it from him?—she had said, "Darling, I think it's time you traded the bucolic for the alcoholic."

For her part, Campbell now desired all things clean and metallic, the cool comfort of a rapid elevator, sunlight flashing off panes of glass and metal birds where once there might have been made gargoyles, high above the streets. Gargoyles did not belong in America, she thought. Sheep did not belong in the middle of a city that all the money had spilled out of. Or perhaps they did belong, in their melancholy bleating, to the collapse of civilization. Campbell was quietly impressed that starving people did not eat the sheep in the night. Some restraint, she decided, must remain in the mad pavilions of Manhattan.

The club was heavy with noise, and pleasant burning and juniper came to those who could pay for it and keep the secret. Over the gin she watched a mutating nimbus of cigarette smoke. She wondered: what secret had Varnas been staring at on the meadow in Central Park? Were his thoughts like her own? "The detective," Campbell said, returning to the subject that she had, from caution, let drift in the cab. She had not dared mention him in the elevator, even though she and Charles were quite alone. "The little man in my imagination has been following for the five years since we were in Cairo."

"How will I know him, if he's real?" Varnas enquired, picking amusedly at the pink flesh of his salmon. "This detective knows something that I don't remember."

Campbell had tried before to envisage the precise nature of the blank space in Varnas' memory. Yes, he was a murderer who did not know whom he had left dead in the dunes. If he were to remember, it would be the death of them, figuratively, or—She was not sure what she thought, if she were able to be honest. And yet, he was getting closer to it. Her terrible aspect even flirted with the idea of telling him everything, just to get it over with. As Campbell saw it, she suffered—perhaps—more than Charles.

"He's rattish," she improvised. "He wears wire spectacles."

"Of course he does." Varnas sipped his gin, relieved. "He sounds quite sinister. Like he belongs on the radio."

"Don't be cavalier, Charles."

The words broke in him. He hesitated, pensive. "What did you say?"

"I said you were being cavalier about my being followed."

Varnas laughed. It was as though she had touched his memories with her strange telepathy and had named what haunted him in what haunted her. *O, my chevalier!* His own ghost…Yes, he thought. He could decide to believe that it was only Knight that haunted him. In a moment of silence, Varnas thought he understood it: He had not killed anyone in the desert. It was a story he told himself to hide his own injuries, the dozen deaths of his childhood. This dread of a crime he could not even see was the feeling merely of shame and guilt that he suffered under Knight. The corpse in the sand, it must be the schoolmaster, he thought, a fantasy of revenge. That glimpse of murder he had caught by some association on Lexington Avenue, it was not real. His imagination had filled in—had put up—a murder, but he was quite innocent. Yes, there it was. And yet, on another day, it might be the man from his childhood who he had seen running away through a Cairo street. He had wanted to kill that man, also. All of it would return to him, in time.

Swilling gin in his mouth, Varnas shivered with a kind of enervated bliss. He reached into his pocket, retrieved the tightly folded piece of newsprint, and placed it on the table between them, staring at it, his expression a chimera of awe and contempt. How it had conspired, he thought. How it whispered his immortality. It was in the poems he carried with him, also. Yet, did he dare believe in it? It could be that a curse was upon him, and Campbell, also. No, he did not want to believe that life—that survival—was punishment. Was it all in his mind? Glancing from the white-draped window, down toward the massed and starving street, he murmured his conclusion. "Look at what we have done with our imaginations…" How would it be, he wondered, to jump?

"Charles, are you alright?"

He straightened in his seat. "I think you may have just performed an exorcism, Campbell." It was glorious to feel the alcohol hollowing him out, the kick of its silver spurs pricking his insides, tilting his head in its aching bridle. That sense of unease he felt had been identified and disarmed. "Whether you intended it, or not." He looked at her, questioning. His mood had shifted. "Say, how about some of that caviar? I feel obscene."

Campbell drank. He had come closer to it but missed. She swooned subtly in the confusion that blooms when a threat is removed unexpectedly. Something had intervened and set itself between Varnas and a catastrophic remembrance. It couldn't last. Dr. Wolfowitz had described such memories to her before. For a few weeks after returning from Cairo, five years ago, she had missed her appointments because she felt liberated, but she had gone back to him. Now, she had not been Wolfowitz's patient in more than a year.

Wolfowitz had kept an office in Chelsea, accessed by a loud and shaking elevator, a tall man in his mid-fifties, dressed always in black, with a silk bow tie, as though for evening. He wore round spectacles, with one of the lenses blacked out for the sightless right eye. Sometimes, these screen memories were fabrications, or fantasies, he had said. One past memory hid another more primal behind it. She understood that all of that was temporary. But now she wondered, could the childish past interpose itself with such force between a man and his consciousness of something that came after it, in adulthood? Beside the common arrangement of layers regressing, could the present slip behind the past? Could one of Charles' psychic screens be out of order?

Whatever the mechanism, she reasoned, it was for the good that only one of them should remember what they had done in Cairo. They might not hang her for it, but Charles—For how long would it last? Would it survive the detective? Her telepathic insight into Varnas' unconscious was insufficient. Or did her talent exist at all? What she wouldn't give to glimpse whatever arabesque shutter had come down like a guillotine in his mind—

They descended an hour later, into the swirling dust of Lexington Avenue. "I feel grand," Campbell said. "Don't you?"

"Oh, very much."

"I wonder if there's a matinee we might catch?"

Varnas said, "All right." He felt good and amenable.

They were about to cross 42nd Street when someone screamed. Campbell turned.

Varnas grabbed her elbow.

"Jesus," she said, and pressed her palm against her lips.

A woman stood at the edge of the sidewalk, bending over as if to vomit into the gutter. She wore a gray woolen coat that clung to her shins, postured as she was, over low patent leather heels. Varnas saw the sunlight flare from a diamond earring, her stricken face in profile, red lips drawn back in horror, gray hair shifting like steam. In her right hand, she held a thin leash. The leash was tight and led at a low angle to the undercarriage of a Chrysler sedan where something was bleeding. Noticing the glint of the earring again, Varnas noted that at least she had not needed to pawn her jewelry, whoever she was. He was only vaguely ashamed of himself for being superficial. Later, when other perceptions fell apart, he would wonder which part his drinking had played in his reactions. "Come on," he said, and turned Campbell away.

Campbell glanced over her shoulder several times, searching either for the woman and her dead dog, or for the Egyptian detective. Campbell pictured him again, like some exquisite phantom. The angles of his face suggested tiger's eye quartz, or fragments of opium. This time, he wore a handsome white linen suit, his hair slick as tar. He was more forceful, lately. Only rarely now, in the daylight of her guilt did he resemble the disheveled creeping creature that she could have stolen from a nightmare. She

relinquished both images after two blocks at East 40th, a torrid
current of pedestrians filling the space behind them. Thin trees
projected from the sidewalk. Someone had studded the twigs with
dollar bills, and many of them had ripped in shreds when they were
snatched, leaving evil little leaves of green notes. Someone was
spanking a child. The cries made her feel queasy.

"Did you see the shanties in the park, yesterday?" Varnas
asked. "All those plywood hovels coming out of the mud?"

"Yes. It'll be the same in Bryant Park, and all over soon."

"People starving."

"Yes."

"The wasteland has found the city. It always does, I imagine."
He thought of minarets broken like eggshells, masonry falling like
clotted blood, ancient scaffolding breaking away, and a vast column
of dust rising over the yellow earth. "I'm sorry, I don't want to be
bleak. I thought it might be distracting to talk, but when I opened
my mouth, all that came out."

"I don't mind," Campbell said.

"One dark thing brings the rest of the darkness with it."

"That woman and her dog."

"Or the new, ninth planet." He glanced at the sky between
the buildings. "You know, it's six months since Planet X was
announced. All these omens of something, the strangest fragments
conspiring. Your sense of being followed. I don't like it." He
could not hold it off. Perhaps, he thought, all of these were caused
by some power in the one he had killed—

The force of this disappointment, the collapse of his self-de-
ception was overwhelming. Varnas' body moved through the
autumn streets of Manhattan, as though shell-shocked. He had
been mistaken. His reprieve had been temporary, some illusion
in the alcohol. The memory of his body bent over the desk while
Knight hung over him like a falcon was only part of the conspiracy of his being. Yes, the assault had happened, but that was not
all. That awful memory could not hold back the slow returning of

the other. The Adversary was coming back to him. The indistinct image of the murder glimmered in his awareness, a scarlet throat gaping under a perfect blue sky. There was nothing he could do.

Campbell did not look at Varnas. She sought for the edges of his psyche, trying to work her way inside his thoughts, probing his disillusionment. They walked between the glass facades of the buildings, the swarm of pedestrians, and the scrawny trees. At a newsstand, she slowed to see the cover of a pulp magazine— *Amazing Stories*—with the painted image of the Chrysler Building lifting like a rocket from a city aflame, a man in a dark suit watching it in despair. Another, called *Wonder Stories*, depicted a woman in a torn white dress caught like a moth in a thick web and man firing a pistol at a bright, gigantic spider. *Vogue* had an illustration of woman at an open window. Varnas lit a cigarette but failed to offer her one. At her side, she sensed that his shoulders were trembling. He put his hand to his face several times. Had he started silently to cry? Was it, she wondered, from some sense of their guilt?

The universe, she thought—that is, her father—had worked hard to instill the due sense of guilt within her. She was not supposed to exist. It exhausted her to contemplate the ways she had found to harden herself against it. She had become so accustomed to it that, occasionally, some rare and conventional fragment of childhood surfaced. These might have been the moments in which he forgot himself and loved her, inadvertently. Yet, his anger unraveled on her like barbed wire in the wind. It had come to her gradually, a gathering of resistance, but it was some time before she met Charles Varnas that Campbell had resolved to be more than the object of her father's loss. She remembered trying to escape the house in the Hamptons for the first time, finding the doors locked against her exit, then her mattress burning on the beach and electricity passing through the wire of her wire bed frame, her small body heaving at the ceiling. She searched her recollections for some indication of the moment when her father must have decided that she might be useful to him.

They had been walking for several quiet minutes after the newsstand, and it seemed to Campbell that Varnas had recovered. He had his defenses, also, she thought. It was too dangerous for her to demolish them in an instant. She suspected that these episodes were evidence that he was approaching knowledge of their crime, of their vengeance against Rafferty Oran Campbell. She must be patient, yet. Charles was not weak. The Devil would never have approved of him, otherwise.

CHAPTER NINE

BREAKFASTING AT THE ALGONQUIN, Campbell folded her newspaper nonchalantly over her knee and yawned. "They executed Panzram, last week." She inhaled deeply again. The muscles at the back of her neck were stiff and tormented by a poverty of sleep. Reaching for her coffee, the cup rattling on its saucer, Campbell looked around the room, at the seawater velvet drapes and the oriental carpet, the cream lampshades, and the cruel electric bulbs. Whatever the decline and doubt outside the red hotel, all of the white-clothed tables were occupied. Abstract piranha faces split the miasma of early morning cigarette smoke, revolving in outbreaks of aggressive chewing and vulgar laughter. Like a German painting, she thought.

Varnas glanced up from stirring sugar into his coffee. Campbell appeared to be framed in a splash of marigolds and snapdragons from the vase on the table behind her armchair. Even in her hangover, she was beautiful.

Campbell drank from her glass of orange juice and asked, "Will you come with me next month, to the cemetery?"

He stared at her.

"Not for Panzram," she laughed.

Naturally, Varnas would not countenance the thought of her going there alone.

In the interregnum, when they sought distraction in the scar-let-bricked shops and speakeasy darkness of the Greenwich Village, when they shared different hotel beds after the last spit had fallen from the last tolling saxophone bell, everything conspired with Campbell's apprehension—the gains by the Nazis—the shivering and slouching of the market—her monthly bleed—running out of ice—Planet X—the unexpected presence or lack of hangovers—Charles being late—the fate of Governor Roosevelt's objection to the Eighteenth Amendment—Charles arriving early—a photo-graph of Mussolini on horseback—the full moon—an airship burning on a French hillside—birdsong—did she appear older—to whom? Yet, the days passed, and Campbell determined not to succumb. She listened to Street and Smith's *Detective Story Hour,* finding the sinister intonations of The Shadow amusing, prepos-terous. She read Blavatsky's *Isis Unveiled,* and Crowley's *Moonchild.* She and Varnas drifted through the city, she remarked one after-noon, like Dante and Beatrice in the underworld. "My sometime analyst once told me that there's a broken planetoid named after Beatrice," she said. "That's rather romantic." For his part, Varnas lived those brief weeks with a hollowness. He did not dare hope for the visit to the cemetery to conclude in the way it would.

Shadowed with sultry oak, its walls waxed with webs of ivy, the green slope of the graveyard overlooked the Hudson. The graves seemed to Campbell to exhale and sigh toward the glit-tering river, and the tug of the mournful boats. She and Varnas arrived early that morning of October 18th, and as they passed through the iron gates, the weather was fine. On that morning, she was no longer anxious. Campbell had resolved to live in the present against all intrusions. She told herself—in a blank Eastern manner—that this, being the only moment, was the best of all possible moments. If only she could have been honest with herself, she would have admitted what a gauzy, laissez-faire defense she had erected against her contingency and how careless, how dangerous it was to ignore the past, but it would suffice for the present hour. The pale graves attested.

No, in the hardness of her psyche, she knew better. Psyche—that great white asteroid, more than one hundred icy miles across, observed by the same Italian astronomer who had seen the fragment named after Beatrice—moved unsentimentally, implacably through the drifting debris of being. Campbell reminded herself that she was no Beatrice. The only demand she made of herself was to negotiate this tangled anniversary with some semblance of honor. Her mother would have wanted it. Yet, she thought, what trash. How could she believe such a thing, pull such gross sentimentality out of the void? She could not afford sentimentality, with so much at stake.

Varnas walked beside her through the graves and their lichens, and she hung on him with her arm hooked through his, going like a pallid blonde saint to the gallows. Pigeons made soft sounds in the trees. The grass was bright with dew, and birds came down to stud the ground with their muddy beaks, searching for worms. The scent of the soil, the grass, and the fallen leaves was almost like silverware in a wooden drawer, Campbell thought. Boughs the color of tar against the sky filtered the morning sunlight, setting scratches and stripes across the plots. As they walked on, between the marble slabs and statuary, the foliage receded from the tended spaces. It was strange to think of the cemetery as exclusive, another place for which there was a price of entry, when time had its claim on everything.

"Do you see them?" Campbell asked. "Some of the recent stones, Charles…October Twenty-Fifth, the first week of November, Nineteen Twenty-Nine. It makes you wonder." Then, she could not help watching for the epidemic of stones from 1918, from the sweated sheets of Spanish flu, and the mud and mucous of the war, corpses missing limbs swimming in dumb tides of blood.

Finally, there it was, the stone with her father's name and the date, one year ago. The breath caught in her throat, and she halted on the narrow path. At Varnas' encouragement, she managed to break the membrane of her anxiety, and approached the grave slowly, still holding to his arm. Then she released it, paused again, and walked, slower yet, over the last two feet of ground. Kneeling on the grass, she admitted the cold dew reaching into her bones. Campbell understood that this was not reverence, precisely, but a kind of occult gesture that was native to the nerves. Charles Varnas knelt with her. Earlier, it had occurred to him that they might bring something, in the way that others would bring flowers. Should they not bring flowers? No, he thought, that was absurd—God, how awful were the adversarial fits at the end.

Campbell stared. The shape in the ground, the black death in the box that had been her father—diminishing with every moment, the remnants of his flesh gnawed by rain—was craven, a trickster possessed with a demon's singular, scavenging cowardice. It seemed impossible that he retained even the shred of courage required to stay dead, to lie in the soundless soil, perhaps listening entertained and content to the ticking of an insect, the coffin's melting velvet, or the worm's gentle process. Before the headstone, she envisioned him looking back up at her, down there with his hair tenebrous as the timber of a burned house, the wry good looks that marked him, self-satisfied and vanishing like a child waving from the rear window of a car in the rain. Where had she been when her father and mother had gone out on their yacht, off East Hampton? With whom had she been left? Could it be true? Had she truly been set alone on a blanket on the stony beach with the silver sky? How had her mother really gone into the Atlantic? Had her father killed her mother before taking her out in his sailboat or did he kill her once out on the water? Into these lacunae, she had lowered more than one barbed hook of self. It was a terrible thing not to know. It was a crime, she thought. What she sought was some reverberation of love, of remorse, or reason for her suffering. And had she not, in her own desperate manner, tried to become the son her father had wanted? The ground was blank.

There had been a moment in Venice, those five years past, when she had looked over the side of the gondola she rode with Varnas, studying in her imagination the fantastic coral of the accreted sprawl of bubonic bones. It was then Thomas Mann's Venice, the puckered and diseased flesh and the matted brown weed of sunken prayers. But the canal was an impenetrable mirror and returned only herself.

Now, the earth was thick, and the coffin lay like a solitary domino in the suck. They lost track of time. Their legs cramped. The Hudson River moved. Campbell picked up a small stone from the grass, rolled it in her palm like a seed, and dropped it into the silence. The silence rippled out from the world until it found the limits of the Sun and the hollow precincts of space where something new had been discovered. The grave spoke merely of abandonment. Campbell wondered, had he ever been there?

When they left the cemetery, Campbell kissed Varnas' cheek. "He's gone," she said. "We may be rid of him." The gothic trees were benevolent to her now. The creeping ivy eased its grip on the bricks of the perimeter wall, and they walked down toward the pewter midday Hudson—recollections of the pearl days when it had frozen over. "I thought if I found him…But I just wanted him gone, somehow. Isn't that strange?" Varnas disagreed, and said it was right.

CHAPTER TEN

IN THE OCTOBER OF 1912, Mr. Knight had called on the Varnas
family. It was the evening before Charles would travel with his
father and mother to Cairo, his first visit. His father was advancing at last, turning his hard-bitten tenacity from the tenements to
the trading company, dragging free of the glue of his class and not
without a sense of loss. He was still adjusting to the incongruity of
it all, of how reading a few good books to better himself and after
drinking accidentally with certain men in a pub—he had impressed
them, and they met several more times in his grooming—he was
to take up a foreign post with the Suez Company. He would give
up his job as a newspaper journalist. Richard Varnas was compact,
intelligent, broad shouldered, and dark beneath the eyes, like
his mining ancestors. He had educated himself, and was being
rewarded, or so he told himself.

Beneath his umbrella, Knight cocked his hand and fleetingly
considered that he should not intrude, that it was too much of a
risk. But he needed to see the boy.

At the knocking, Richard Varnas—fatigued from packing
up the house—buttoned his shirt and palmed his black hair. The
evening was full of sleet when he opened the door to Mr. Knight,
whom he found waiting patiently in the pour of moonlight, his
umbrella humming, one sleeve of his coat drenched through. It was

an unexpected visit, but what could Richard Varnas do and not appear ignorant? They had only spoken on school grounds before. He felt momentarily that he was being inspected but forced that guilty sense of himself away. The schoolmaster supported the leg that had shattered when he fell from his fox-hunting horse with a black, brass-hilted cane. The two men greeted one another, and Knight was invited in. Charles' mother, an apron still worn over her lilac dress, wiped her hands with a dishtowel and said that she would have tea for them, momentarily. Mr. Knight closed his umbrella and Mr. Varnas took it from him, setting it in a metal bucket inside the door, ushering him inside. His cane made a sharp tacking on the wooden floor. Knight could not resist glancing up the dark stairs to his right. He stepped painfully into the living room where Charles was seated at the small table where the family ate, pretending to read a week-old edition of *The Daily Citizen* that had come in the post to Oxford from his father's friend in Manchester. As Knight appraised him, Charles was still dressed in his white school shirt, gray shorts, and hard scuffed shoes over gray socks. The boy had removed his school tie, but otherwise looked the same as he did during the day, dark hair in need of washing, a sulk in the lips, those sad eyes like the English Channel. There was a recent scratch on the boy's face. A piece of bread and butter lay on the bare table.

"Most of the house is packed up," Richard Varnas said, indicating that their guest should sit in the armchair close to the fireplace. The bulky furniture would remain for the next tenant. With his new posting, this might be the last time that the Varnas family were tenants and not owners. That would be something else to get used to, he thought. Would they return to Manchester after? He was not fond of Oxford, but he went where the work was. "I'm surprised there's any newspaper left for you with all the packing, Charles. Put it up now, lad. We've Mr. Knight come to visit."

"Hello, Charles."

Mrs. Varnas returned. "The kettle's on. It shan't be long." Her face was very white. In the kitchen, she had tied her brown hair back.

"No trouble, Mrs. Varnas."

"Call me Audrey."

Knight inclined his head and smiled. "Audrey." Still seated, after unbuttoning his coat, having gone urgently into the living room without removing it, he picked up the poker from the grate and stirred the coal embers. "You don't mind if I—?"

"Not at all. It's bitter out. Get warm." Mr. Varnas was only gently resentful of the ease with which the schoolman had settled himself in their home. "We didn't expect you. I hope we have enough cups not wrapped in newspaper for tea all round."

"How are the poems coming, Charles?" Knight said, finally succeeding in shrugging off his coat.

The boy shook his head and put his hand to the reddish scar that ran from his right eye socket to his ear. He could not admit that he had thrown all of his poems into the same fireplace where Knight now stretched and rubbed his cold fingers. Everything he had ever written was gone. If there had been the promise in his poems that Mr. Hulme—the quiet, too ambitious collaborator whom he also wished dead—had seen, all that originality was betrayed now.

"I came to give something to you."

"Will you take Mr. Knight's coat, Charles?" his father said, as though his son had forgotten an elementary courtesy.

Charles got down from the table and retrieved the coat from the outstretched hand of his adversary. Did he seem to retain hold of it for a second, like an argument between them, before relinquishing it? From inside his gray, cable knit cardigan, Knight retrieved the package he was keeping dry. Charles saw it after he had hung the coat in the entryway, beside the umbrella that dripped into the bucket.

Accepting it, Charles unwrapped the gift from its brown paper.

"The poems we shared," Knight announced. "Read them on your way."

He had no choice but to acknowledge it politely, but his voice was soft, and unsure. "Thank you, Sir."

"And there's space after, for you to put your own poems in it. Come here, let's look at it together. One last time, yes?" Knight opened his knees, as if the boy should shuffle back between them, and kneel there, letting the dangerous man read over his shoulder.

This, Charles did, and the fireplace embers burned close to his bare legs. He was afraid, as he had been before, and resented the way his father smiled as if the scene was a pleasant one. How could he know? Someone—he—should speak up for the child. Charles could not stand to think of his father in the way he might think of Hulme, as a dull-witted collaborator.

"Here's the tea." Audrey Varnas brought the service on a painted tin tray—the same round tray that Charles had ridden in the snowy northern streets of the past, spinning like a dervish. He hurried to help her now.

"I'll give Dad his cup," he said, adding sugar and stirring. His father sat at the table, since Mr. Knight had the chair at the fireplace.

"I'm very proud of Charles, Mrs. Var—Audrey. If I had a son, I would very much hope he might be like yours."

"You have no children, Mr. Knight?"

In her accented voice, Knight's name was pronounced almost like "gnat," Charles thought.

"Alas, no." He shook his head and looked at the fire. "Mrs. Knight took sick—cholera—before we could begin our family."

"I'm sorry to learn that, Mr. Knight," Richard Varnas said. "We're truly grateful for your care and interest in Charles. It's a shame to take him away, but with the posting—"

Charles felt sick. Could no one see what was happening, and what had happened to him?

"I envy you, Charles, going to Egypt. I should like to be there. Oh, you'll see the great pyramids, and the mysterious Sphinx! Although," he caressed his broken leg, "older, I go on three legs now, as the Sphinx predicted." He smiled, insinuating. "Perhaps I will see you there, one day."

Charles saw himself holding the teacup and saucer in two
hands as he had in Knight's study, but leaning close to his father,
this last of the unpacked good china rattling as he whispered what
Knight had done and had been doing. In the distant silence of his
rage, his father would stand, approach the fireplace, take up the
brass poker, and smash the schoolman's skull with it, bringing it
down in a vicious and righteous arc, the lurid blood whipping
across the wall—*gash gold vermilion*—Then, he would push the
raging furnace-forged tip into his Adversary's heart with a terrible,
infinitely satisfying hiss. But the boy Charles Varnas could not
speak. Later, when he thought of his parents from the vantage of
1930, he thought of the warm northern brass in their voices. He
wondered if, like Mr. Hulme, some Mancunian affect was still in
his voice, however faded, escaping the likes of Campbell whose
American ear was not attuned.

A week later, the Varnas family was in a strange and sultry country
with palm trees and imperious, lion-watched bridges over a river
that seemed to be everywhere like a dream in his young head.
He was fascinated with the sloppy camels, the shrouded drivers,
and their unfamiliar burdens. At the bookstalls, he studied the
dark-skinned men with their expressive hands and quick-spoken,
swooping language.

Richard Varnas' office with the Suez Company was brocaded
with tobacco smoke, coffee, and sweat. Charles Varnas would
recall the impressive and colorful map that covered most of the
white plaster wall opposite the window that looked onto the street
below, close to Victor Tiring's new department store and a brief
walk to the Ezbekiya Gardens. He was too young to fathom the
work his father and the other men did in the offices, one floor
above the street. He knew only that he liked to be there as they
went about their arcane business, smoked cigarettes, rolled their
white sleeves, and spoke loudly and urgently. His mother would
sit near the window and read a newspaper, folding it to fan herself

when the heat flowed through the city like an invisible tide of lava. He would sit there with her on a small, slate-colored steamer trunk with stiff brass fastenings. There were days when a gramophone played, and these he understood to be successful days for the Suez Company and his father.

A year later, his parents were dead. From the seething street, a Bedouin threw the grenade that killed them. It came crashing through the glass where his mother was. It should have killed him also. Varnas could not see how he had survived it. His father had been working at his desk, his shoulders hunched over a collection of receipts as though he bore them in a wheelbarrow. As usual, his mother was reading beside the window, her legs crossed, one shoe dangling and bouncing on her toes. Charles was seated close to her on a low stool. He was reading. The fierce rays of the sun reddening his bare legs, tilting his memories of England. The windowpane next to Audrey Varnas had smashed and a heavy metal cylinder fell onto the tiled floor, rolling like a bottle on thin grit before coming to rest against the wall with the Company map. Momentarily, the bomb seemed to ring in the sunlight. His mother cried out and pointed to a man, running away below them. Charles stood and glimpsed the man's flapping ivory burnous, a youthful, yet weathered face with heavy-lidded oval eyes. Charles turned away from the broken window to the thing against the wall—the explosion, vivid as the sun, blew a swarm of shrapnel through the room.

He could not hear anything. There was a mass of smoke hanging over him, reaching into his lungs, trying to pull them out. The white wall and the map were gone. Only a few stubs of plaster and wood remained. A small fire burned on the broad desk. His father must have stood up and tried to shield his mother from the blast but had not moved in time. Both of them were sprawled at grim angles, motionless, covered with shattered floor tiles and rubble. Their bodies were scorched and shredded. A ragged section of the ceiling had fallen, and someone was shouting down through the hole. The boy looked helplessly to the man, whose mouth was as panicked and soundless to him as a decked fish. Charles Varnas' body shook, the concussion of the grenade estranging his atoms, setting his organs in an alien shivering under his ribs, beating his brain against his skull, setting the destroyed room in a nauseating series of fluttering stills. Almost imperceptibly, the sounds of the blown world returned to him—ringing bells—shouting—a telephone in a distant room—His emotions failed him, for he had no gauge for this horror. Years later, he would be able to say that he experienced himself as a boy hollowed out by terror and grief. He would at last inhale and realize that he was still holding the notebook that Knight had given him. The effects of the bomb faded, and he sensed that he was uninjured. The image of the Bedouin, running across the tram tracks returned to him, pedestrians stepping aside for him, then closing behind him. This man with his pale shroud—his features so ghostly, yet so watermarked in Varnas' consciousness—he resolved to kill.

CHAPTER ELEVEN

1925. THE TURQUOISE WATER around the gondola was frigid where Campbell traced her fingers, the boat black and curling like witch's rib. Traces of soft green algae clung to her carmine fingernails. She reposed against a scarlet bolster, one lithe arm hanging over the dark boards and testing the chop of the channel. In that attitude, wearing her new sunglasses, a white blouse, white trousers, and tan loafers, Campbell crossed her right leg over her left and regarded her companion, as he gazed pensively at the azure sky as if something might fall and obliterate the scene. How different, Campbell mused, was this sky to the one that had witnessed her mother's drowning? Behind her, their hook-nosed gondolier in his straw hat sculled the shallow boat in the direction of the Piazza. The noonday sun struck her as hard and metallic. Campbell discovered that if she reclined against the red cushion, her trouser leg made an agreeable pale slash across Charles Varnas' seersucker suit. He had just told her something terrible, but something in the vague evil of the inundated city left her unable to respond where she might. It was hard to sympathize with other people's memories and exhausting after a time. Sometimes, they imposed upon her, unbidden. Campbell turned to watch her shadow warping over the iridescent film of the canal. She loved to think of the surface tension of water. It was an image of the surface tension of being. It was easy to drown. They passed beneath arched stone bridges where their gondolier would bend at the waist and lift his hand to run his fingers against the cool masonry. Finally, Campbell summoned her sympathy and said, "That's—"

Varnas started to speak at precisely the same moment and seemed not to have heard her. "All I could do was to stand there, holding the book limply in my hand as though I was dangling a wounded bird by one wing. The shrapnel from the grenade had not touched it, either—Christ—me and it, unscathed. Eventually, the Company returned me to Oxford with their bodies." He put one finger to his lips. "And I was mute for an entire year."

"You really didn't—I mean, really you couldn't speak? From the shock." Campbell wondered how much of the conversation the gondolier could understand, as though he might remember this strange couple, and might endanger them with the police one day. He oared impassively, dark wrists weaving in the salty, seaweed breeze. It was too late, she supposed. Campbell heard Varnas' confession patiently, indulgently.

"One of those religious philanthropic groups—I suppose that's what they think they are—got hold of me and sent me across the Atlantic, because I was an orphan now. They would take lost ones and scatter them like seeds across the soil of the Commonwealth, some to fall on stony ground, some to find the good. There were about two dozen children, some very, very young, disgusting really, who were sent with me on the ship to Canada—probably all turned into bloodshot farmers' boys or prostitutes in Whitby for the fishermen or the railway workers. I managed to get away from them. It's strange. You know, I forget the name of the family I was being sent to, perhaps because I couldn't say it out loud. I don't know. Anyway, from some waiting hall in Toronto, I absconded around dusk, before they could come and collect me."

"You just bolted. Running, just like that."

"Yes. It was a bitter night, winter, and black as all hell. I might have died, I suppose, but I couldn't think of that. And besides, recent experience told me that I would manage. I couldn't speak, and I might as well have been blind. I didn't know where I was going, just running away. I don't recall being scared—And then, my darling, like a miracle the sun rose on Niagara Falls, and I got my voice back."

"At that very moment?"

"Indeed. I cried out for my parents. The cataract was covered with ice, and the undercurrent flowed beneath it, falling into a white fog at the base of the cliffs. For a long time, I watched the ice melting in the brilliant sunlight, and I turned thirteen in America." He watched her, the shining of her green eyes, the glimmering of the canal, her alabaster skin. "There," he said. "Now you know how I came over. No secrets—except those we make together."

"Charles," she said, resting her left hand on her abdomen.

"I believe this is our stop."

That afternoon, on the Piazza, a knot of desultory, bow-legged children attended by a nun fed purple-gray storms of pigeons. Campbell wanted to know why the children appeared so sickly. Varnas thought it must be from rickets, and that they had come over from the Lido on one of the larger passenger boats. He said that he had read about that in a guidebook, somewhere. St. Mark's Basilica was reminiscent of some undersea palace, golden blue coral accumulating pale and porous spires, crucifixes like rosy fishhooks, accreted arches of sand, minarets of air-filled dolphin skin. Varnas guided Campbell in front of it, away through the mass of tourists toward the bell tower where they would climb. The paving shone from the receded tide. Spare fronds of brown weed dried in the sun. A viola player dressed something like a bullfighter shouldered gently between the cafe tables. Campbell smiled at Varnas, linked her fingers with his and squeezed. This intimate gesture distracted him from the uncanny sense that they were being followed. The brush of her slim hip against his, set Varnas' blood alight like gasoline.

"Look there," Campbell said. "That's the same architecture as the building where my father has his business." Campbell pointed at the colonnade and pyramid three hundred feet above them on the bell tower of reddish stone. "Yes, that's it! You see, the Bankers Trust Company Building plagiarized this campanile. Let's send him a postcard. Taunt him just a little." Varnas picked one from a wire rack and paid for it. He could picture the building back in New York, on Wall Street and Nassau; she was right. The bell tower looked new, having been rebuilt twelve years ago, after its collapse, something else he had read in a guidebook. Reaching inside his jacket, he plucked out the notebook that seemed to have saved his life like a fetish. The ribbon that had once kept his page had come away. Lately, he had taken to fastening a small pen to the book with an elastic band. He pushed the pen into the blonde hair behind Campbell's left ear. "Wonderful! We can write to him from the top," she said. "I have stamps back the hotel. We'll mail it before dinner." Somehow, she did not care about the risk involved. It was merely that she wanted the provocation.

They climbed the narrow stone steps. From the belltower, Campbell stared between the white columns, out across the Grand Canal to the promontory of the old customs house, an ivory point projecting into the beautiful water. It reminded her of a miniature painting of the southern end of Manhattan, except for the chaos of red tiled roofs. Above their heads, the great bells hung, black funnels of silence. Above these, she regarded the sea-green pyramid of the spire. She took Varnas' pen from behind her ear and began to write. He put his arm around her waist and watched the water under the transit of the pale sun. Everything was pleasant and tranquil. Perhaps it was the high vantage. Being away, he thought, did that.

They did not mail the postcard immediately, returning instead to the mad luxury of the Hotel Danieli, their gothic palace on the darkening lagoon with its spits of black boats and tilting lanterns.

There, they would dine on room service of sardine bigoli. From the landing stage they had entered a sprawl of crystal chandeliers, Moorish stained glass, soft damasks, orchid-white plasterwork, arabesques, blood-red staircases, marble columns, and oceans of oil paint in gilt frames. They decided to take chilled champagne on their moonlit balcony.

After, Campbell undressed and reclined naked on a chair upholstered in green velvet, her legs spread over each turned golden arm. In the illumination of the moon, her scars came out, evidence of many failed exorcisms. Kneeling, Varnas unfastened his belt. He closed his mouth over her, breathing the fresh sweat in her hair, his tongue seeking inside her for the satin sourness of her pleasure. Campbell took his head in her hands and pulled him tighter. After she had rippled and shaken against his lips, he took her wrists and pulled her on top of him, sprawled on his back on the intricate Egyptian carpet. Campbell corkscrewed onto him, and held his wrists in turn, pinning him, her hair like wet straw across her blushing face, her knees reddening, her small breasts against his skin, as he pushed himself up into her. When she felt him starting inside her, Campbell breathed heavily, "You're my moth, Charles—My moth—You're my damned and darling moth."

At midnight, Charles Varnas stood naked on the balcony that overlooked the silent lagoon and smoked a cigarette. Campbell was asleep, a thin white sheet draped over her narrow body. Beside her, there was an empty champagne coupe on the chinoiserie night table, and the postcard to send to her father. Rafferty Oran Campbell was fond of him in a limited way—This he knew. Something rogue in each man had met and agreed. It had been a compact of sorts. He knew that it could not last. He searched himself for the moment when this had occurred to him—An image of Campbell sketching horoscopes on a restaurant napkin. That early? Inhaling the cigarette, Varnas thought of how the rich man's daughter had pinned him to the carpet. Pleasure streamed through him, again. How he had half-surrendered to her, fixed, yet struggling with all his sex to raise her in the silver-blue light toward the Dionysian fresco on the ceiling.

Yet now he recalled the way Mr. Knight had held him down, the gray, snide schoolmaster's cruelty and manipulation, dishwater eyes, the pain in his childish innards, the faints of tea and Vaseline, and now this gorgeous, ambivalent girl—What important thing was she to him, too great for expression?—His childhood returning?—The wild vengeance of the boy that could not speak? The thoughts came to him and oscillated against all his will, each image a glassy tile demanding its shining place in his conscience, whatever that was. Briefly, he stepped back into the room and groped around for an open bottle of Chianti, before returning the dark overlook of the lagoon. He drank from the bottle. The wine was good. Somebody was weeping in the next room. He could not have said if it was a man or a woman. Now, there was no moon. He studied the stars for familiar constellations, but found none—

CHAPTER TWELVE

FIVE YEARS AFTER VENICE and Cairo, the night before Hallowe'en, 1930, Campbell set out a new constellation. Above the empty, drowned rooms her father had bequeathed her, in the echoing mansion that overlooked Central Park, she returned to her solitary rituals. It was, she reminded herself, a matter of not giving in to fear. She lit the creamy candles in their green skulls on the mantel. For some time, in their decadent glow, Campbell stared at her denuded self in the snake-framed mirror. She knelt in front of the grate. Campbell had undressed half-way through her second martini and her third Lucky Strike. With a heavy brass poker, she stirred the embers and fragments of coal. The orange surge of the flames scorched her legs.

She had spent the day at the library, lost in ornithological watercolors, a moth-eaten pamphlet on satanism, heavy tomes of Egyptology and astronomy, gathering the disparate facts which her intuition insisted were necessary. Crawling to the rug in the center of the room, she found the single tarot card she had set there as before, but already face up, known intimately—there was no point pretending suspense. The rug was prepared with her pentagram of ash. She entered the consecrated angles without disturbing it. Kneeling comfortably, she appraised the objects she had collected. Beside the tarot card was the tightly folded column of *New York*

Times newsprint that she had retrieved from the table when she last dined with Varnas at the Chrysler Building. He had lost concentration from the gin, and she had slipped it into her sleeve. That was no deceit, she thought. She had only sequestered it from Varnas because he thought he understood it and had no more use for it. Had he not said something like that?

Campbell put her fingertip to the five-year-old postcard she had never sent from Venice. It described how they would continue to Egypt, and how the gondolier with the hooked nose had been delightfully suggestive of peregrine-headed Horus. Arranged next to these were notes about a child named Venetia she had written at the library on a scrap of yellow paper. In Campbell's alcoholic glamor, the underworld echoed. There was a beauty to it, a mad resonance. All this, she contemplated through half-lidded eyes, feeling for alignments in her altered state, describing the way one thing reached for another, intimations of purpose, streaming chills of recognition.

Campbell smiled and unfolded the newsprint report on Falconer's lecture on immortality. Had she not warned Charles Varnas to be careful with time? Her breath came steadily—Slowly—Then pushed by something—She closed her eyes—And the fragments emerged like stars from the pagan pitch of night—the New Planet—Planet X—Pluto—named that spring of 1930 by this girl named Venetia Burney—Like Venice—Twelve years old, now—in Oxfordshire—Granddaughter of Falconer Madan—

Campbell started. There was a sound close to the fireplace, as if something had fallen from the mantel. Something entered the indistinct slice of her vision. It was small and white, and it moved toward her by some weird volition. She managed to open her eyes fully long enough to watch as Rafferty Oran Campbell's monogrammed golf ball rolled toward the orbit of pentagram, and then came within it, crossing unnaturally the slightly raised lines of ash.

"You—"

In horror, Campbell shut her eyes again, the pressure setting red lights pulsing under the lids.

"—can put your clothes on, now." It was a low, Irish voice. "You've got the poetry of it, I'll give you that. And yet," the voice insisted, "a few well-placed coincidences can fray the mind." It was a vicious sound. "Ask Charles if you don't believe me. But I think you've noticed, already. You know, since May, Herr Doctor Jung—the poor bastard—has been calling it 'synchronicity.' That's quite nice, isn't it? Synchronicity—That's what he sees in things like your cards, your silly spells, and their correspondence, all that paranormal bullshit."

Campbell could not look at him, but did as she was told, rising, staggering, covering her eyes with one hand, groping about the room with the other, struggling to get away from his voice. Her fingers, as she worked at the buttons of a long black silk shirt, betrayed her. There was an interval of cold silence in the room before he spoke again.

"You won't look at me, girl, while we speak?"

Giving up, leaving the shirt undone, Campbell shook her head.

"No? That's disappointing."

Against her will, she began to weep uncontrollably, choking on mucous, pressing her face violently into her crossed elbows at the mantel, afraid to glimpse him in the mirror. She had forgotten to cover it, and now he was there, fully. He was stronger than she had anticipated. She wanted to scream but could not. Her throat was riddled and sewn shut with thorns.

"I agree with you, girl. I think Varnas really is quite close to remembering. And when he does, what then?"

She managed to whisper, "I don't know."

"The interpretation that he has, his conclusion cannot hold. He has already undermined it. Just as the Nile has its banks, denial has its limits. And now, all the banks are—broken."

"Not yet," Campbell said. "What do you want?"

"Child, what will you do when the money runs out? It is going to run out, you understand? You must know that. Do you think he'll stick around, someone like him? Once an orphan parasite, then always—Jesus, with his proclivities? Caviar, gin…It can't last, can it? And now, I'm not only talking about the money."

"Stop it."

"Aye, you might just be that stupid, girl. Shall we consider our position? Curious how Pluto appeared just after the Crash, as though your beloved Planet X was just latent, lying in wait, you might say—"

"Please—Please go."

"Does the name Bennu mean anything to you?"

"Please—"

The telephone rang.

Immediately, Campbell sensed his absence, and opened her eyes. Grabbing the mouthpiece, without waiting for Varnas to speak, she said, "Come over, now. Hurry." Buttoning her shirt, she picked up the clipping from the *Times*, the Venetian postcard, and her yellow notepaper from the library, and dropped them each into the fireplace, stirring with her poker until the flames consumed them all. The monogrammed golf ball, like a miniature planet, she returned to the mantel. "Bastard!" Finally, Campbell took the rug to her French windows and shook the ash over the balcony. He was trying to drive her insane. When Varnas arrived, she would be dressed and made-up. Rain caressed the windows as she combed her hair.

"How did you know to call?" It was gone midnight when Campbell admitted Varnas to her home. His bleached hair was wet.

"Hi, Campbell."

She took his raincoat and hung it in the hallway. Beneath his coat, he wore a simple white shirt with the sleeves rolled, and gray trousers flecked with rain.

"Sorry, it's wet," he said. "The cab broke down a block away." Varnas walked about the living room, drifting past the mantel without regarding himself in the serpentine mirror. The two white candles remained lit, and their flames set his shadow vast against the William Morris walls. He inhaled a pleasant scent of incense, something like pine. Varnas relished the bohemian aspect of her living room, the rugs, and the obscure books. It was an atmosphere that relaxed him instantly and made him feel that he was in an alien place. That alienation was luxury. "So, are we having drinks?"

She hesitated for a moment, and despised herself for it, for succumbing even for a moment to that insinuating voice in the dark. "Of course. I'll fix. Really, how did you know to call?"

"I don't know what you mean. You called me."

"Oh, God," she laughed. "Brandy?" She retreated into the kitchen and returned with two glasses.

"Sure, that'll take the edge off the night. But, seriously, are you quite all right? That's a good fire you have going for this time of night."

Campbell handed him a drink, the amber rolling in its large bulb. Her dark shirt flowed over a pair of matching trousers. "Do you remember the woman with the dog?"

"Yes, how horrible. It's haunting you," he suggested, kissing her cheek.

She inclined her head, angling her eyes from his, and sipped at her drink. "You said that one dark thing brings another. Yes?"

Varnas grew self-conscious. "Well, I was in a dark place that day." He drank a little and sat down on Campbell's seal-brown Chesterfield, the leather creaking as he crossed his leg. "Harbingers of—"

"Yes! And then you said something about 'the ninth planet.'"

"It's called Pluto."

"I know." Campbell pressed, tenderly: "But it was as if you were upset by it, also."

He struggled for an answer, not knowing what he should say to help her, shifting momentarily in his seat like a cornered animal, then drinking again. It felt good and loosened the knot of his doubt so that he exhaled with assurance, the louche dignity that alcohol

loaned him. "I suppose you can't get much darker than that." He
hesitated, again. The brandy worked in him, reminiscent of the
fierce needles of the Sun. "Well, look, I don't know about myself,
but I knew that it interests you—Astrology—A new planet coming
out of the darkness surely has to upset the map, distort the future.
And there it came, perhaps small and cold, like a period at the end
of being. Or a frosty searchlight, come to discover everything. I'm
not sure what I mean, I suppose, but I felt it." He tilted his drink
in its glass. "I'm confused. What are you getting at, Campbell?"

"I'm not sure. Is it an omen, like you said, a precursor to
something worse to come?"

"Some other intruder? You tell me. It might be meaningless."

Campbell reclined against him on the sofa. She wanted to tell
him what had happened to her but could not. It was too ugly. The
fear had diminished but had not abandoned her. She could not say
if she would explain it to him in the days to come, whether the
issue would be forced by further contact, or if she was losing her
mind. Varnas would be inclined to believe her. That was its own
rationalization for her silence. She finished her brandy. He finished
his, reached for the bottle and poured another.

"I'm glad I called you."

"I love you, Campbell."

Campbell drank. The words came unexpectedly on an exhala-
tion, regardless of her will. "He's back, Charles."

"Who is?"

She was as stricken and strange now, he thought, as she had
been that night at Khaled's bar. "My father, the Devil."

—After Venice, they had taken the train west to Milan and then
south to Genoa. He dreamed of the Lanterna lighthouse probing
the purple dusk as the ship put out. The sea was rough in the main
channel, and the ship drew close to the coast. Campbell stood
with him at the rail, cold spray in their faces, she with a glass of
Sangiovese. He was in a good mood. She nudged him with her

elbow. "There!" She pointed at the lights on the coast, unconsciously tilting her glass so that a blood thread of wine spilled into the black waves. "Viareggio, where Percy Shelley's body found the beach."

Varnas had inhaled, wondering how many times the sand had turned over and been sucked away by the waves. At the thud of tide against the green hull, Campbell gripped his arm. He had dreamed of spectral seagulls weaving off the stern, over the white lace wake, Naples, Palermo, Malta, to the North African coast, the ambiguous sound of weeping in the next cabin during the night—A nightmarish return to Suez in the raw heat of the day, cranes, rusting shipping containers, and brown oil slicks clotted with dead birds. Always, the feeling of being watched, resented—

She slept heavily, her head in his lap, with Charles Varnas dreaming intermittently in his dog sleep of their transit to Port Said, five years ago—In the violet hours of the next day, Varnas shrugged gently from beneath Campbell's sleeping body. He found himself thinking about Campbell's detective, trying to fill his outline in his mind. Varnas was still dressed, having spent the night slumped in the corner of Campbell's sofa. He had managed to kick his shoes off, at least. The fire was almost out, but stubborn embers cracked and glowed like pin pricks of orange and white. He went silently to the hallway, letting his eyes adjust to the deeper darkness there. Locating his raincoat, he twisted it until he found the bulky pocket. Returning to the living room, he knelt at the fireside grate, holding the notebook. He did not notice the absence of the news clipping. The leather was cool at first, but quickly drew the heat of the ash and his need until it felt like flesh. If he concentrated, even in the gloom, by memory of the shape of the words that he had read a thousand times, he would be able to read the handwriting. He opened it, hopefully. Immediately, he made out "A Soliloquy of One of the Spies left in the Wilderness." Furtively, scanning over it as though it were a forbidden thing, a blasphemy, he read—

A press of winged things comes down this way
…

He turned the page.

He slew the Egyptian yesterday. To-day
  In hot sand perilous
He hides our corpses dropping by the way
  Wherein he makes us stray.
…

Sure, this is Nile: I sicken, I know not why,
  And faint as though to die.

Shutting the book aggressively, yet conscious of not waking Campbell, he thought, *God damn you.* It would take so little, and yet so much, to press the book into the satanic dunes of ash. So, he held it there, hovering over the heat. Soon, the leather was sticky in his scalded fingers. Yet, he understood that if he were to drop it, it would not be gone.

"What is it, Charles?"

Varnas withdrew the book, and the burning of his skin asserted itself in stinging, angry pulses. Standing, he turned toward the Chesterfield where Campbell had propped herself up on her elbows. Varnas smiled. "Happy Hallowe'en."

CHAPTER THIRTEEN

THE COSTUME PARTY TO which Campbell and Varnas were invited
was on the 9th floor, at the well-appointed home of the actor
Milton Konigsberg, at 1 West Sixty-seventh Street. The syca-
mores and oaks of Central Park hissed in the breeze as they crossed,
dressed in black leather coats, carrying their beak-like masks. Under
the gargoyled limestone facade, Campbell turned to Varnas to kiss
him. Then, looking carefully at the tall building, following the
lines of the stone, she said, "I was right, Charles. Gargoyles have
no place in America." The blunt faces stared back, worn down
with weather.

They reached Konigsberg's door at 10 o'clock. Before they
could ring the doorbell, it was opened by a waxy-skinned,
red-haired young man dressed as an English butler with a white
silk bow tie. With unfeigned deference, he presented each a glass
of champagne from a silver tray and admitted them to the riot
inside. Their drinks were each prepared with a thin paper straw.
Konigsberg had instructed the young man in all things. Before
announcing their names to the other guests as best he could above
the cacophony, he should address each guest: "Enter freely. Go
safely and leave something of the happiness you bring." Almost as
an afterthought, unpracticed at parties as he was, the butler offered
them ivory cigarette holders engraved with the date. He cupped

his right hand to the side of his mouth like a megaphone and announced them, "Ms. Campbell and Mr. Varnas!"

Although she had not visited in a year, Campbell knew the tall, five-room suite well, the actor having been a friend of her father. All of the homes in the building were opulent, imitation gothic, like movie sets with grotesque chandeliers and yawning fireplaces. Konigsberg's place was filled with a miasma of cigarette smoke and ecstatic noise. Campbell turned to Varnas, lifting her glass. "Drinking straws," she laughed. "My God, Milton thinks of everything." A figure Campbell intuited to be a disguised Milton Konigsberg drifted toward them through the torrid chandelier and candlelight. The chandelier had a thin cord dangling from it, and the butler's pulling on this would keep it swinging slightly all night.

Milton Konigsberg was dressed as all of the invited guests had been instructed—and as Campbell and Varnas were—as a plague doctor in a long leather coat that skimmed the floor, a white beak mask with inset eye lenses like the tinted goggles of an arctic explorer, and a broad-brimmed sable hat. Konigsberg had told Campbell that the Crash was like a modern Biblical plague, and something must be done to drive it out. "The rivers are blood," he had said with melodrama, "and the first-born are dying. Soon we'll have nothing to eat but the locusts." Several uninvited guests had arrived as witches, harlequins, Mayans, pirates, and chimeric animals. They could be of no assistance in this ritual.

Varnas' raven-black mask stood out among all the white versions. In a leather-gloved hand, he raised his champagne glass and slipped the paper straw into one of the two breathing holes on the underside of his beak. Campbell watched his champagne vanish into it. Among the countless plague doctors, it was like being lost in a mad flock of birds. Konigsberg leaned between them, lifting his mask a fraction to greet them and to conspire. "Say, don't let on or everyone will demand one, but there's a small sponge soaked in laudanum in the tip of my beak." Konigsberg laughed, the drug bending him at the waist. Then, he stood straight, gathered himself, and spoke loudly above a skipping jazz record. "How are you Campbell? Delightful to see you, Charles! So glad you could make it!"

"Thank you, Milton," Varnas said. "This is really something!"

"I invited precisely one hundred friends. All were to wear the same costume style, but as you can see from the misfits in the wrong garb, there must be one hundred and thirty in here by now, but who cares? Say, test out your drinking straw, Campbell! They have a wax coating that'll preserve the paper for about an hour. But for God's sake," he laughed again, "don't drink that slowly!"

"Ingenious!" Campbell said.

The main room with its staircase to the library was a parliament of beaked figures in heavy black coats. "It's like a plague convention," Varnas said. The effect was overwhelming.

Campbell was delighted. "I adore it, Milton." She tilted her head back to watch the sway of the chandelier overhead, the frosty aurora it cast against the ceiling and the walls.

"Let me show you where everything is," Konigsberg offered. "And by *everything* I mean the bar."

Varnas clapped him warmly upon his leather shoulder. "Let's go."

Campbell whooped and took Varnas' hand as they made their way through the tight, Black Death coils of the party.

"Here it is." Briefly lifting his mask again, the better to be understood, Konigsberg indicated the hatch of a dumb waiter in his cramped kitchen. "Ring the bell once and cocktails come up. Ring twice, and you can use this notepad to write any requests to send down. Sometimes, there's even food that arrives. Help yourselves or let the help bring it around, it's all the same to me. You can send empty glasses back down, too." Konigsberg was manic. "Oh, God, I shouldn't have even suggested that. Please don't feel compelled to do that. Everything will get cleaned up, eventually. It's pretty quick. Let's check on that music, anyhow."

They went with him. The gramophone was to the right of

the fireplace, where a flock of plague doctors had assembled to peck at the silver-framed publicity photographs and playbills on the mantel. "Ah, this is my new favorite," Konigsberg crooned, his voice eerily distant in his laudanum beak. He adjusted the needle. "Louis Armstrong. 'Body and Soul.' It's brand new."

"I like it," Campbell said, swaying in her heavy coat, ivory beak, and black hat. She had finished her champagne, and taken up a martini, with a new paper straw. "This is a terrific party, Charles. I think we needed it!"

Milton Konigsberg bowed and retreated toward the door where more shadowy figures surrounded the red-haired butler like carrion birds.

Varnas took up a martini of his own, again pushing its straw into his breathing hole. "This is great, but I think if I try to smoke in this mask, I'll drop dead and ruin everything." He wrapped his arm around Campbell's hips, and their beaks chapped together.

"Here," she said. "Did you see this?"

"What is it?"

"He framed it, the gruesome devil! Then again, I think I might, too, if I lived here." Campbell handed Varnas a section of newsprint behind glass, set in a silver frame.

He read the headline aloud. "COUPLE SHOT DEAD IN ARTISTS' HOTEL. SUICIDE COMPACT IS INDICATED BETWEEN HENRY GREW CROSBY AND HARVARD MAN'S WIFE." Sipping his martini, he continued, "*Henry Grew Crosby, 32 years old, of a socially prominent Boston family, and Mrs. Josephine Rotch Bigelow, 22 years old, the wife of Albert S. Bigelow, a post-graduate student at Harvard, were found dead about 10 o'clock last night—*" Someone, doubtless Konigsberg, had scrawled a date in blue ink across part of the line but motive is unknown. It was dated December 11th, 1929. He had also annotated it to record that it came from *The New York Times*. "*—each with a bullet wound in the head, in the studio apartment of Crosby's friend, Stanley Mortimer Jr., a portrait painter on the ninth floor of the Hotel Des Artistes, 1*

West Sixty-seventh Street. The couple died in what Dr. Charles Norris,
Medical Examiner, described as a suicide compact. The police believe that
Crosby, in whose hand they found a .25 Belgian automatic pistol, had
shot Mrs. Bigelow and then turned the weapon on himself…was described
as a poet…nephew of J.P. Morgan…"

"Do you think Mortimer is here?"

"God, I hope not. Not with this thing on display."

"What possessed them? Or him, really. I remember it, from
the news, but I forgot it happened here. The cops broke the door
down with an axe." Regardless of the truth, Campbell reasoned,
the dead couple were on that side of the Crash ledger that could
call them its casualties. The music picked up and several of the
guests began dancing.

"Immortality—" Varnas voice was muted in the weird beak
mask.

"What?"

"It doesn't matter. Let's find a bite, okay?"

Campbell could not have said when she lost Charles Varnas in the
crowd that churned in Milton Konigsberg's large living room with
its tall starlit windows and tilting chandelier, but when she looked
back over her polished leather shoulder, she did not see his odd,
black mask, only the mass of white beaks, and someone dressed as
a mummified corpse in worm-eaten bandages, an imitation police-
man, and a middle-aged vampire with white-streaked hair and a
red-lined cape among the intimate conspiracies of drunken plague
doctors. There was a second gramophone in the room now and
the two struggled discordantly like alien plants, howling metal-
lically. She called his name and repeated it. For a moment, she
thought she noticed him, close to a woman in a green dress who
had fixed rubber snakes in her hair with fishing line. Campbell
grew afraid. She needed Varnas to protect her from the presence
that had visited her the night before. It was almost too much. The
strain of repressing it left her nerves thin—A glimpse of a grinning

tanned face under black plastic sunglasses and a ratty red fez, pale linen shoulder turning aside—

Then, he was there. "Campbell, are you okay?"

She embraced him. "Charles! I want to leave. Is that all right with you? I don't want to be a bore."

Varnas laughed. He glanced cynically at what he suspected were other couples who appeared exhausted but determined to last the party out. "Of course," he said, a little drunk. "It's not like we paid a babysitter." He lifted their wooden beaks and kissed her. "Sure, sure. Screw it. Out, out. We can go in just a moment." Varnas searched frantically for a last martini to drink on the way through the crowd to the exit. He intercepted the red-haired young man who was passing delicately toward two plague doctors and a dismal satin Pierrot whose ruff was stained with red wine, as though tuberculosis had struck the clown some time earlier that evening. Tossing the straw and the olive aside, he lifted his mask and drank the gin in two fierce, relieved swallows.

Without speaking of it, they intuited that neither felt the need to seek out Konigsberg to make their excuses. Varnas was pleased to be able to slip away without more straining to be heard. The alcohol was pleasant in him. It made him feel that all things were possible. He felt relaxed and powerful.

Hesitating in the hallway, Campbell and Varnas examined the closed doors of the other suites for indications of repair after the policeman's axe, or any entrance that appeared incongruous and new. Standing outside it, the party was still terribly loud. Campbell went from door to door, like an unquiet specter. Varnas shrugged. There was no longer any sign of the doomed couple's suicide pact. Campbell was disappointed.

CHAPTER FOURTEEN

THE NIGHT WAS COLD as they crossed Central Park West and drifted solemnly under the lambent trees at the perimeter toward the meadow. Campbell reached her black-gloved hand for his, and they gripped one another with the fingers of people drowning in a bitter tide. Charles Varnas realized that he was still holding his empty martini glass and felt a small guilt for stealing it from Konigsberg. He rested the glass upon a park bench for someone else to discover. Certainly, he thought, the actor could afford to lose one. For a time, they walked without speaking. The sheep had retreated to the north-east of the receding pasture, but could yet be seen, white and silver in the press of darkness, huddled and motionless as a photograph of smoke, or a mural of clouds, he thought. He wondered if the painful association they had set in him previously was used up. He seemed to be able to see them without memories that night. Perhaps this was an effect of Hallowe'en, a kind of suspension of pain. Campbell paused, pointing toward a row of plywood shacks. There were about a dozen small shanties, collaged from whatever discarded material and waste that could be found and nailed or lashed together, cardboard, painted planks of splintered signage, corrugated metal, tarpaulin shreds, and dirty bedsheets. They moved toward the row of makeshift shelters. There were obscure objects scattered in the mud that had spread about the small buildings.

"Welcome to Melanesia," Varnas said, ironically. "They call these Hoovervilles."

"I feel like I'm in the proper dress." Campbell knocked her wooden beak against his. "Look, Charles, there's a light in that one."

In another abysmal shack a child was weeping quietly, and someone was trying to comfort it. Varnas pulled Campbell on toward the glassless window and the guttering candle she had pointed to. As they approached, it seemed that another candle was being lit inside. It was the last shelter on the row.

Time out of joint, the two figures—leather coats dragging over the rippled mud and embedded trash, wide hats eclipsing the distant streetlamps, their grotesque conical faces and glass eyeholes— moved through the acrid smoke of a dead bonfire.

"They got killed of the sheep," Varnas said. The tortured, partly stripped skull of a white ewe stared from one jellied eye socket in a dune of ash. The soft flesh of its cheek had been peeled crudely from the bone with something blunt. Half of the tongue protruded from the side of its smashed jaw.

Campbell whispered, "Oh, God, how horrible."

"Let's go on."

"Someone's awake in there," Campbell said. Again, she hesitated.

"Of course," he said, casually.

At the smoldering fireside, they were almost directly outside the shack when the flap of corrugated metal that served as its door shifted. It seemed to Campbell that the occupant struggled with it as if it were stuck in the dirt. Then it fell outwards. The displaced air sent white ash and red sparks into the night. A figure staggered out.

"Feh!" The man was tall and dressed in a suit that appeared in the moonlight to be rusted with filth. There were smears of what Varnas took to be oxidized blood on his cuffs. Seeing Campbell and Varnas, the man cried out in a projected whisper, trying not to raise a full alarm immediately, "Nein, nein! Please, we don't want any trouble here." He pointed back down the row where they had passed. "There's babies." From his pocket, he retrieved a pair of round spectacles with one lens blacked out.

Campbell was aghast. "Professor Wolfowitz?"

He squinted at the beaked faces. "Yes—Who are you?"

She removed her mask.

He studied her for a moment. "My God, Campbell! What are you doing here?"

"That's not the point—What are *you* doing here?" Campbell removed her gloves and put her hand on his filthy shoulder. After the party and without the disguise, the freezing air struck, needling at the rim of perspiration where her mask had been. Wolfowitz was pitiful, bent. Campbell pushed her gloves into his hands. "These are too small for you. Give them to someone else. Charles, give Professor Wolfowitz yours."

"Naturally. Here." He removed his mask and gloves and introduced himself.

"Thank you, Mr. Varnas. I think I remember your name." Wolfowitz tossed both pairs through the hole in his shack where the metal door had rested before it fell. "I'd invite you in, but the maid hasn't been."

Varnas said, "Campbell mentioned you, but it's been a long time, hasn't it? Take this also." He threw his sable hat inside the hole between decaying plywood that was the doorway. Without these, he had only black trousers and white shirt sleeves against the chill. It didn't bother him. It was the same for Campbell. They stood before Wolfowitz, beautiful and blond in the ashes and excrement where the commune broke like a wasted wave against the meadow.

Wolfowitz squeezed the coat in his soiled hands. "I lost everything. My savings. My clients. My apartment. I tried to walk out of the city, but gravity, you know. I was pulled back, even though there's nothing here. I walked a lot. My loss, the collapse of the market, it was very fast. Very fast. Like a torrent."

"You have family? You were going to go to them?" Varnas asked.

"Not in this country, alas, and for good. But I did get a sheep tonight." He stooped a moment to place the coat inside his shack, and to retrieve a claw hammer from beside his filthy mattress. "Got it with this!" He seemed to see the gore and fleece hanging from it for the first time and crouched shamefully, trying to wipe the blade in the mud, coughing violently as he did so.

Varnas wanted to ask the analyst if he'd ever treated Crosby the suicide, or the girl. There was a smell of putrefaction beneath the last coils of the bonfire smoke. There must be another dead animal, he thought, or more concealed somewhere in the gloom.

At least the child had ceased crying, Campbell thought. She did not know what to say next. Later she would lament this, and her selfishness, knowing that it was a false silence. At a loss, Campbell shifted on the balls of her feet. Then, she remembered. "I have something. Do you recall how we used to speculate about Planet X, all those years ago?" she said. "They found it. Did you know that?"

"Oy, no! That's incredible. A miracle!" Wolfowitz wheezed. "I shouldn't make so much noise." He glanced along the squalid row of improvised dwellings. "You said they would discover it at the right time."

"Yes. Yes—" It would have been quite simple for her to offer Wolfowitz some money, but she did not. She did not because it would run out, inexorable as a clutch of sand, and Charles could not know. She wondered if this sudden consciousness of her money would last, or if her carelessness would return as soon as they were out of sight of Wolfowitz.

"Surely, we can help you. Even just a little, right Campbell?"

She did not move. At last, sensing Varnas' unease, she spoke disconsolately. "Perhaps the children can play with the masks."

Varnas opened his wallet and handed Wolfowitz a ten-dollar bill.

Wolfowitz inclined his head.

Varnas glanced at Campbell, inscrutable in the night. "Perhaps we can come back."

Inhaling and holding her breath so that she would not have to breathe him in, Campbell made a single step toward the man with the black lens in his spectacles and embraced him. "Goodnight, Herr Professor." She palmed his shoulder, gently. "Goodnight."

Campbell was several paces away before Varnas could react and hasten after her. As he caught up with her, he heard Wolfowitz dragging his warped metal door upright, and closing himself inside his shanty for the remains of the night.

"What is it?" Varnas caught her arm and walked beside her, east across the sheep meadow toward the lights of Fifth Avenue visible between and above the trees. "Did it bother you that I gave him money?"

"Was it your money to give?" Campbell snapped.

"All right." They made several more paces as he looked for the moon, behind a purple nebula of clouds.

"I'm sorry, Charles. Perhaps we will go back and see him again. I don't know. It's just—"

"It's horrible, I know, to see someone brought low like that. You knew him before, so it's an impossible—"

"Yes. That's it."

Varnas understood that he had run himself to ground, cringing under the thorns of recollection, his face flushed from flight. Like a pack of dogs, his memories encircled him. The first visits to Knight's office, when everything was innocent, when he received only that crucial charity from a kind man with his silver hair, his dishwater eyes, and his brittle tea set. What had set the change in? How far had he himself been responsible? The spike that twisted its shock up his spine, sprawled on the desk with all the tortured poems—the smell of himself, present as an animal—his quiet tears and snot— Knight turning away to wipe himself with a pale handkerchief— tea leaves swirling in the brown pool at the end of his cup—Have you ever heard of divination by leaf, Charles?—No, Sir—It's called tasseomancy. Would you like me to read your fortune in

the leaves, Charles?—I'm afraid—Recollections of watching the
hunt entering the trees off Foxcombe Road, close to Boars Hill,
the heaving horses, pack hounds, and the men in their red coats,
white jodhpurs, polished chestnut boots, and black helmets, and
the trees whispering in the barking and the horn blowing mist.
And the time after that, following, watching. And the time after
that, predicting the arrival. Setting his trap for Knight's horse, the
twist of its massive brown body, the snap of leather, and its rider
falling into the rooted mud. The horse halted at a patch of grass,
illuminated in a gray beam from the wintry sky. Varnas remembered how it had been to be this boy—His adversary, his tormen-
tor unconscious in the forest. Standing over him with a mossy
rock in his fists, sharp under his fingers, but hesitating—hearing
the dogs again—The break of ravens from the covering oaks—
Varnas had watched the blood spilling from the white thigh where
a stiletto of creamy bone had pierced Knight's skin. Varnas had let
the stone fall from his grip and watched it roll away from the soft
incline of dirt and brown leaves where the schoolmaster lay. And
he ran away, his heart repeating through the cold boughs, in every
bark, howl, and call. He did not, at first, notice that a long spike of
hawthorn had cut deeply into the skin close to his right eye when
he ran. Later, he would think about how he had nearly lost his eye,
and how that might have implicated him. Varnas remembered that
it had begun to snow as he breached the trees and returned to the
slope of roadside where he had left his bicycle in a tangle of ivy and
decaying leaves. And then it struck him how beautiful the place
had been. He was too far away now to capture it, but he wished
that he had managed to sit down there and write a poem about
just how beautiful the place had been, once he had destroyed his
enemy. Arriving home, wishing he had brought the jagged rock
down on the limpid face. He should have killed Knight then—

Now, Campbell and Varnas came to a place where they had been
ten years ago, in the January of 1920, when the winter had been

vicious, and the pond had been frozen over. This was where they had met one another. People had skated on the ice. Here, Campbell and Varnas had each walked their separate perimeters for the last time. Recollecting—Varnas was watching one of the skaters, a handsome figure in a dark woolen coat and a green cravat turning arabesques on the brilliant, scalloped surface. So distracted had Varnas been, that he and the girl almost collided. He remembered her vivid green eyes and the morning light in her Marcelled blonde hair. They stopped and watched the scene together for some moments before each realized that they were watching the same man skating, weaving now between a crowd of children skidding there in their ordinary shoes. The children cried out excitedly, falling into one another.

"My father would seem to be in his element," she had said.

"Born to it, I'd say," Varnas replied, smiling. He removed his knitted cap revealing hair as jet-dark as the skating man, picked off his gloves, and held out his hand. "Charles Varnas."

She had removed her gloves, also. "Campbell."

He could not have known then that he had been sought out, chosen. He did not know then that his life had not been his own for some time, that the agents of tragedy who had intervened in his life were elements in a fatal design. A week later, the trinity of Varnas, Campbell, and her father ate a fine steak dinner and Campbell plotted their horoscopes on a napkin—

Now, they stood there in the Hallowe'en night, after the close of that decade when they had been brought together, and the beginning of another. "I knew you, immediately," he said. Campbell squeezed his hand. She said that she did not want to spend the night at her place, "this night of all nights." The effect of the party, of the shanty town, and of discovering Wolfowitz derelict in his hovel had disturbed her. Since, in ordinary times, as part of their arrangement, they only lived together when they were in hotels, Varnas was pleased.

PART THREE

"Those who go beneath the surface do so at their peril. Those who read the symbol do so at their peril. It is the spectator, and not life, that art really mirrors."

—Oscar Wilde, *The Picture of Dorian Gray*

CHAPTER FIFTEEN

CAMPBELL RESTED HER CHEEK against Varnas' pale chest, recollecting the way that in Egypt the sun had burned a rosy angle where his collar opened, and listening to the haunted thump of his heart. There was fathomless pain in that restive tissue. She put her fingers to her wrist and tried her own pulse, found it thin and recessed, as if it had turned inward against the horror of being, against the mediocrity of survival. She thought of Géricault's *The Raft of the Medusa* with she and Varnas the only ones left after the leer of cannibalism and madness of the wide, wild water. Charles, she thought, had loved Paris more than Venice, Florence, or any of the Italian cities they visited in that spring of 1925. The Louvre fascinated and appalled him, the intriguing Egyptian inscape of death in the hollows of the modern city, and the ancient masks of gold, and painted wood, the statuary and the bones preserved. She remembered an image from somewhere else, a print of Napoleon on his horse approaching the Sphinx. It had been at the Campbell estate in East Hampton—her father must have chosen it. How lonely that place had been. It was as though she had lived like a hysteric, shut away under the bitter auspices of her father. Yes, there were things that she had found a means of forgetting, also. She and Charles had that in common. That was pleasant, in its way.

In Paris, she and Varnas had sought out the spiteful, violent gestures of the Dadaists and the strange, somnambulist psychology of the Surrealists—both being vital to Charles' sense of himself. Yes, she thought, he was tough in his strange way. Turning her head on the pillow to look at the window, did she recall that Duchamp had lived close to Konigsberg, in the same building, above or below him? The window shades were open to the lights of the avenue. She thought of suicide pacts, a young woman with a hole in her head, a man missing a plate of his skull. She became lost inside a vision of threadbare poltergeists looting the broken windows of the department stores of the city—She had no single, stable thought, only a beaded corona of flares from the lovely eclipse of gin, the impenetrable resistance of her conscience. Abruptly, her drunken consciousness dropped, and her awareness of Varnas' bed distorted, tilted under her hips, leaving her faintly nauseous. Pitching on agitated waves of alcohol, the same strip of anemic architecture and screaming stars repeated like a flickering half-turned page. The remorseful sweat of the night meant that Campbell would not sleep until she was utterly dissolved in her crucible of exhaustion.

For his part, Varnas suffered impassively beside her. Like a scratched record, his first sight of Niagara Falls—scraping himself through that mute and frozen night—played over and over behind his clenched eyes, borne on the racing tide of his blood. He saw white floes and floods cataracting from a vast glacier—the glacier an interplanetary dream. He was strangely bereft. He wanted to cry, yet his flesh failed him—was it all insincere? Did he pretend? When his father and mother had been murdered, what if he had not been rendered voiceless? What might he have said, between the orphan ship and his escape, between the Nile and Niagara Falls? How does revenge become a word?—Campbell—There was nothing else for him. He went dimly toward her position in the florid heat of the stars. She was a private religion. She was a comet dragging him toward oblivion. She was his understanding of God and Devil. The flesh took over—the semen against the inside of his thigh—the ache of his ribs beneath his heart—the impending headache from the twin ropes at the back of his neck, working, taming against the eternal pleasure of his knowledge—falling beneath the endless ice—

Osman Raffi came to Hooverville dressed in a pale linen suit and a blood-red fez, chewing the arm of his celluloid sunglasses in the corner of his mouth where they lolled like a giant locust. He favored cologne but wore none that night. He went sober and lean through the trees. He had tailed Varnas and Campbell from Milton Konigsberg's Hallowe'en party and ghosted his way across Central Park West. His brown monk strap shoes had been silent as Nureyev on the asphalt. Avoiding the streetlamps that would have rendered his suit in a phosphorescent fuzz against the murky facades of the avenue, he passed into the park. Such was his arrogance that he preferred the difficulty of tailing in such stark dress. Assuredly, Raffi shrugged and shifted, until he reached the shanty town that was as thin and brittle as the abandoned skin of a monstrous snake. He lingered close to one of the shacks, not touching the soiled sheet of cardboard that worked in imitation of a closed window. Muted at first, a child began to cry inside, squalid, the tone familiar to his memories. The sound the child made was born of the pain of hunger. It had nothing to do with his shadow passing across its existence. Keeping his clothes clean, he disdained any surface beyond what he had picked for his shoe soles. Osman Raffi watched and waited.

He saw the couple ahead of him speak with a man of about fifty years of age, his own age, whom he would soon learn was a down-and-out psychoanalyst and carnivore named Wolfowitz. He strained to listen. Regrettably, the despair of the starving child obscured most of the exchange, except what sounded like a suggestion that the couple might return to this scene. Varnas, he saw, had given the man some money. Through thin smoke, he observed also how they gave him their plague doctor costumes and witnessed the perfunctory, awkward manner in which Campbell embraced him at the end, as though this impoverished place was also a leper colony. His mind worked over the costumes. Soon, he knew what to do. After Campbell and Varnas had gone, he waited yet another twenty minutes, motionless, cramping in the posture that the moment and its scuffed terrain dictated. Here, he had time to consider the scene at Konigsberg's party and its miserable pretensions, all the silvertone vanity of his photographs, the excess of alcohol, and the dumb, defiant money. At last, without a noise, he loosened his wiry muscles and advanced on the derelict.

Slumbering in his soiled suit, Wolfowitz heard a faint knocking at his door of corrugated metal. His refuge was oil-dark beneath its plywood ceiling. His exhaustion was a wave of sand that pressed him down and disoriented him. The knocking came again, and his heart twitched in his breast. Campbell must have decided to return with more money, he thought. On his torn mattress, he rolled stiffly onto his side, feeling for the rusted spring that coiled out of the fabric, so that he could safely push himself up without being pricked and poisoned by it. God, what a fairy tale, he thought. The grass at the edge of the mattress was matted and dying. Wolfowitz groped for the rusted tin that held his candle and the matches. He whispered, "Just a moment, please." Touching his face, he was relieved to discover that he had removed his spectacles before falling asleep. They were on the empty fruit crate next to the ripped construction site sandbag he used for a pillow. He located his socks and shoes and put them on, inured now to the alternately acrid and putrid smell of his flesh. When he rose, the shanty flickered amber, his shadow bloating on the wall. He could not stand to his full height inside. Earlier that day, he had joked with himself that he was back inside the womb. A broken man, like an infant, he thought, is nothing but potential. When he reconsidered this, the thought embarrassed him. It was a boon that he had no one to talk to in that manner, anymore. Taking hold of the short piece of wood screwed to the interior side of his corrugated door, Wolfowitz lifted it an inch and moved it to the left.

In the eerie moonlight, he saw that the man in the pale suit at his door was holding a revolver, pointing it at his face. The man was poised with his finger to his lips to indicate that Wolfowitz should not cry out for help. He wore a fez. Wolfowitz made no sound, but raised his hands slowly, retreating back into the hovel where he collapsed breathless upon the mattress.

The stranger with the gun followed him inside and pulled the door behind him, maintaining his aim at the reflecting bridge of Wolfowitz's spectacles in the candlelight. "I won't hurt you," the stranger said.

Even with his voice lowered, he had an accent that Wolfowitz understood to be Middle Eastern.

Osman Raffi stood over him, his revolver satisfying in his hand, and got the man's name.

Slowly, Wolfowitz drew his knees up to his chest and pulled his elbows in. Now he was in the womb, he thought. He lost some urine into his suit and the awful mattress. He mouthed something and moved his head, his eyes spilling silent tears. He could not control the spasming movements of his shoulders.

"Please relax, Wolfowitz. Nobody is getting hurt. I'm just a detective." He lowered the gun, but it was still aimed at Wolfowitz's exposed torso. "I'm out of my jurisdiction, but this is a matter of—how would you say it?—life and death."

"What do you want with me? I have no—"

"You see, I was with some friends at a party. On the way home, I was distracted, looking at the stars, and in that moment, I lost track of my friends. Do you know the people who came to see you earlier?"

"They didn't know I was here. It was by chance. But I know the girl more." Wolfowitz's voice was thick with mucous.

"Campbell," Raffi said, agreeably. "Yes, she is my friend."

"Yes. Is she—are they in trouble?"

"How do you know her?"

"She was my patient." Still, Wolfowitz's voice was barely above a whisper. Terror of the candlelit revolver kept him in check. "I don't remember her address if that is what you need. I have no files anymore."

"No, I know precisely where she lives, and where Mr. Varnas lives. But I did not know that she had been ill."

"No, no. Not like that. I am an analyst."

"You have a nice office," Osman Raffi smiled. His wide-set, luminous eyes gleamed like oil under a match.

Wolfowitz almost laughed. Something of the intolerable tension in his loins released, and he felt the wetness of his clothes and the bedding beneath him. Mortified, he apologized. "But I have not seen her for a long time."

"How great was her suffering?"

"It's hard to say. I have had more complicated patients. I thought she was neurasthenic."

The detective removed his fez, revealing smooth, pomaded hair.

"By which I mean," Wolfowitz explained, "that she was a woman unprepared for her existence, for what one might call the pitiless structure of American life. It clashes against the psyche. They become exhausted, anxious. Now, look around us. Perhaps the neurasthenics had it right, all along. It's an American disease, you understand?"

It was good that Campbell suffered, Osman Raffi thought. "I'm not a Marxist, however."

"But you did not know I was an analyst, so these are not the questions I imagine are helpful to you. Please, tell me what is it that you want from me?"

"Do you intend to see them again?"

"She—Campbell—said that they could come back."

Raffi's voice was hard and bitter. "They will not."

"What crime are they supposed to have committed?"

"Oh, they are cold-blooded killers, Mr. Wolfowitz."

"I can't believe you."

"It does not matter if you do, or if you do not. I wish merely to understand their associations. You are an associate. But they will not come back to see you. They are for themselves, only. Now, I suggest you close your eyes."

"Please, no!"

"I'm not going to shoot you, Mr. Wolfowitz." He smiled once more, slipping the gun into his trouser pocket. "Did you ever have your palm read? Hold out your hands." When Wolfowitz's eyes had flickered closed, and his hands extended, the Egyptian took his left hand and permitted a tender silence between them. Finally, with all the reassurance he could draw upon, Osman Raffi said, "I am not the Devil."

Wolfowitz kept his eyes closed and smiled nervously.

From the inside jacket pocket of his pale suit, Raffi took a shaving razor and drew it swiftly across Wolfowitz's throat.

The analyst fell back, the cords of his life severed, choking on his blood, his fingers testing the long and pulsing gill that the Egyptian had opened in his dirty skin. From some instinct of protection or dignity, Wolfowitz rolled and put his face into the dirty mattress, so that Raffi could only watch the shallow motions of his back as he lost consciousness and drained into the wadding.

The Egyptian detective said, "But, I am the Devil's devil."

Raffi searched the shanty. He gathered the long leather coats and the plague masks that Campbell and Varnas had worn and took them outside, making thirteen paces before dropping them on the grass. Calculating, he took one coat back for himself. He threw Campbell's white mask back inside the hovel. Returning to the corpse, he found additional candles in the corner of the shelter, the dregs of a bootleg whiskey bottle protruding from beneath the bloody bedding, a newspaper, and a frayed shirt. He lit all of the candles, so that he worked in a circle of them. Alternating layers of paper and strips of shirt, he wrapped the head of the claw hammer and dowsed it with the alcohol, before adding the last drops to mattress where some of the wadding had ruptured out. Touching it with the candle, it flared with a blue light. It was weak, but sufficient. With this hammerhead torch he burned a section of cardboard wall, waited for the flame to find the corpse. It would not have to destroy it completely. He moved quickly, setting the other places alight. The flames passed furiously down the line of shanties, igniting the walls of detritus, the fire dragging the dwellings like the sparking tail of a red comet. Osman Raffi ran to the cover of the closest tree, a broad oak with names scratched into the trunk. From there, he watched the burning, and the smoke that coiled beneath the moon. Of those emaciated figures that broke screaming from the fire, he did not see the child. At the 72nd Street subway, Raffi used a payphone to report the murder and the arson to the police. Should he fail, then eventually, the costumes he laid out in the park would be traced back to the party at Konigsberg's place. That would take time. But Campbell and Varnas would be identified, and a great murmuration of police would come after them through the city. They would be electrocuted or hanged. Yet, he would not fail. He was certain of this—

CHAPTER SIXTEEN

Varnas awoke with the frost of a nightmare on his skin. Campbell slept in his arms, damp and sheeted with it also, gin tainting her shallow breaths. He wondered how he might tally the multitude of times in his life that he had fallen asleep drunk, and how effortlessly he might have died in that sleep, choking on a thin line of vomit with no one to hear the sour languor of his breathing coming to a stop. Or perhaps, this could not happen to him. It could be that he had died many times before— Flat on his back, his arrogance disgusted him so that he shrugged abruptly from the bed, leaving Campbell to drowse in and out of consciousness in the white pillows. He grabbed his robe from the floor and prepared some coffee. In the street below his apartment, the early traffic moved stiffly.

"You have a melodramatic way of rising." Campbell found him in the kitchen, fragile November light filtering through the shades. She had put on one of his shirts.

"How are you feeling?"

She hesitated. "I dreamt about the Egyptian detective. He followed us from the party, and he murdered Wolfowitz. Then he burned all the shanties to the ground. I saw him. And it was our fault."

"Jesus." He handed her a cup of coffee.

"It was as if I was with them, witnessing it, helplessly, unable to intervene. But really, I do think he was at the party. I only glimpsed him, but it was him, without a doubt. And I know his name, now." Campbell breathed across the surface of her coffee, the cup close to her lips, pensive. "Either he has become careless, or he has chosen to reveal himself, just to spook me. His name is Osman Raffi."

Varnas watched her green eyes. "You're serious? You got his name in your dream."

"Quite serious. Good morning, by the way." She kissed his cheek and said, "I think we should go back to the Park today, later, just to see."

"To see Wolfowitz?"

Campbell sipped her coffee.

Varnas noticed a thin tremor in her fingers.

She swallowed and inclined her head, struggling against that part of herself that persisted outside of time. She did not want to consider it now. "Maybe. I don't know. We should also go to Katz's again. The booze has me feeling all hollowed out. Can we do that, eat first? Then I might be able to think straight."

He agreed.

They took some time to wash and get dressed. She applied some of Varnas' cologne and studied his hairline. "You need to bleach again. The dark is coming through."

Varnas said, "I like it this way."

As they descended and stepped onto Park Avenue, Campbell changed her mind about Wolfowitz and the shanties. She must check on them first thing, before she could stomach breakfast. They were both delicate from drinking, but they had forgotten, or had ceased caring to dress for the cold weather. The weather was not that bad, Campbell said, all things considered. Appetite and anxiety flushed her with acid. They walked, she with her head down, toward the squalid place where they had discovered Wolfowitz. She anticipated a strip of ashes, smoldering stubs of wood. The spectral image of Osman Raffi hung over it all, exaggerated and discolored like a poster for a film.

"There. You see, it's fine," Varnas said. "Nothing has been burned down."

She saw that everything was as it had been the night before when they had spoken with Wolfowitz. "He's probably gone out. He said he walked a lot. I would, were I destitute. Wouldn't you?" There in the daylight, she could decipher brand names on some of the cardboard walls, laundry that must have been done in the pond, now drying on improvised clothes lines. Derelict figures moved between the hovels. There was a smell of excrement, rot, and woodsmoke.

"Do you want to go further, see if he's at home?"

"This is enough."

At Columbus Circle, they flagged down a cab. It took them down a section of Sixth Avenue, then across to Fifth and down to East Houston and the red-bricked delicatessen. The men and women who clung to the city went like automata with solemn metal eyes. The cab driver's skin, Campbell thought, had an eerie green stain. For a moment, she imagined pustules rupturing the clammy scalp at the places his cap had made sore. "I think that this Hallowe'en really got under my skin," she said. They negotiated the cement trucks attending the new Empire State site, the building missing sections of its facade, vast girders probing the sky like bloody antennae, the construction teams reminiscent of larvae clinging to sickly nectar over the unfathomable streets. Everything, she felt, was peeling back, exposing all manner of her nerves, probes, suckers, labia, wings, hairs, raw flesh, and steaming viscera. Something was trying to break through.

"They say it'll be the tallest tower," Varnas observed. "But it won't be the most handsome."

The cab shivered like a scarab over the broken skin of Manhattan. Campbell looked at her wristwatch—a Tiffany on a black velvet strap—and found that it was not yet 10 a.m. She thought of her hunger as the permanent condition of the city now, gnawing on itself from the inside. Since the party, she thought, her self-pity had become infinite. If it was the weight of deceiving Charles about the money—and was he even really deceived, or merely too polite to expose her?—she could not say. If it was an effect of the suicide pact in the newspaper clipping—picturing the livid bullet and the girl's resigned brain spattering the penthouse—she would never know. If it was some fear brought out by Charles' perverse intimations of immortality—the pitiful hangover of poetry—she could not decipher it. Soon, they reached the delicatessen and Charles paid the driver who was, now that she looked again, reasonably young, and healthy with a greyhound's reaching face. Inside, finding a Formica table, she ordered bagels and more coffee, scanning the room, her agitation evident. Varnas ordered a Reuben sandwich and coffee.

"It'll be all right, Campbell. It was just a dream, after all."

She watched the faces. "Yes, you're right. Then why should I feel so sad, like everything is going to Hell?"

Varnas considered their position. "Honestly, I think we're both utterly exhausted. I've felt it in myself for some time. And I've come to recognize that there's a very fine line between the sentimentality that swells out of fatigue and the real evidence of sorrow," he said. "One can lose the line. And it's also true that remorse feeds on the weary souls first." His mouth formed a smile that his eyes ignored. "And what have we got to be sorry for?"

Campbell stared at him. He added nothing more. Katz's was hectic, but the crowd was pleasant, the people tolerant of one another's raw edges. Certainly, they were not the only ones present who needed to shake off the intoxication and disturbed sleep of Hallowe'en. Campbell thought of it as a kind of camaraderie, gallows humor, the congeniality in shared suffering. She forced herself to brighten as she lifted corned beef on her fork. The flesh and the brine were delicious to her. "Okay. So, what did you dream of last night, while I was dreaming of the malign Osman Raffi?"

"You, of course."

"Liar." Her green eyes flashed.

"I don't know." He tried to recall something from the obscurity of the night or any night, where the luminous stalks of ice and of peels of snow had bloomed pallid over the stiff drag of Niagara, where his voice had returned to him in a torrent of feeling—something that he could not put into words. "I dreamed that I was young, again. I think."

"That's a nice dream," Campbell smiled. She watched his face as he worked at recollection. Despite the pervasive cold and their carelessness, it did make her happy that they were dressed alike, in the trousers they had worn beneath their abandoned plague coats, and both of them wearing white shirts. "A nice dream. Like something from Oscar Wilde," she said.

"Your father leant me that book," Charles said. Unconsciously, not hearing his own voice, he muttered, "And a few well-placed coincidences can fray the mind."

"What did you just say?" Campbell demanded.

"What? Oh, just how your father loaned me that Oscar Wilde book."

"Of course, he did," she said. "I like it here."

Minutes passed before Varnas spoke again. "I always wondered, if there is no such thing as an immoral book, why Dorian Gray had to die. Are you almost finished?"

"I think so."

Charles Varnas recalled the night that he stood alone on the balcony of the Hotel Danieli in Venice. Campbell had appeared angelic in her sleep, pale as the face of Psyche. He had never told her how the starless midnight had impelled him to dress and walk quietly from the room and out of the hotel. He had lit another cigarette as he drifted like a vampire, west over the Ponte della

Paglia, under the pale wings of the Ducal Palace and toward the
Basilica. Inside, drunk in the shimmering candlelight, he had stood
beneath the Ascension dome where the Son of Man was suspended
in his deep blue starfield, encircled with saints and sceptered hosts,
his mother, painted palm trees extending their fanned leaves, and
the virtues. Varnas had pressed himself onto his toes, eyes fixed on
the golden Christ. There he stood, until the cramp in his calves was
too painful. His throat was strained with a yearning to which he
could not have then given voice and could not now. The distance
between himself and the ascended man seemed infinite. The stone
beneath his feet held him and refused him. Just to have slipped it
for a moment, he thought, to have responded in kind to that gentle
lure of life. If only he might ascend even a hair's breadth—Varnas
had staggered from that place. His blood had hissed in his veins.
The knowledge that disappointment can be fatal was loud within
him. When he returned to the hotel, slipping past the shunting
gondolas in their salted dock, he locked the door to their room
and undressed. He was cold from the night and his sweat. Without
disturbing Campbell, he had settled on top of the sheets and closed
his eyes. The obscure weeping in the next room continued—

"Gorgeous!" Campbell dropped her napkin onto her plate and
gulped at the remains of her coffee.

"What do you want to do now?"

Campbell wanted to walk Bowery and see the queer signs of
the tattoo artists. She wanted to see the latest flophouse rates in
chalk like the signs at the champagne champing racetrack where
nobody enjoyed themselves, the cost of indigestible food, the black-
eyed men with leeches and dirty cotton towels at their sockets, the
loud shambles under the elevated railway—All of this, she desired,
picking their way through the broken glass to Chinatown and the
thick amber in the air to buy a pillbox of white powder from an
old man with skin like dried seaweed. "We won't feel the cold so
much with this," she said. "How did you like the look of those

leeches?" She shuddered amusedly. "We should get you some, Charles. They could live in a jar or some kind of aquarium in your apartment and you could feed them—What do they eat apart from the blood of recent wounds—scraps of meat, flies, or something?"

Wrapped in a stolen leather coat that skimmed the cobblestones, Osman Raffi followed them as they passed before the facade of the building whence Campbell's father had fallen. He watched as Varnas held her hand. He took it quickly as if he were catching her balance. Varnas also caught the glance that Campbell gave the bend and brood of the noonday sky and the precipice where her father had been, as though he could have been in Venice, suspended with a tourist's pleasure over the bright lagoons, the whispering bridges, and the canals of memory. Her father—

At the corner of Wall Street and Nassau, he plummeted into the crown of her head like a prisoner vehement to return to his certain cell. Into that benighted comfort she felt him come. She almost welcomed him. He fell like a coin tied up in a ribbon of black. She had felt it before.

Raffi, light as a hound, was more cautious now, having given Campbell an intimation of his presence. He did not wear his fez, but the brilliantine of his hair was as it ever was. This was a bleak city in the winter, he thought. The day was too dark for his new sunglasses to appear more than affectation. It could be, he thought, that she perceived him walking at this discrete distance from their pale backs, and that she was merely stringing him through the labyrinth of her remorse. Arrogant women like Campbell would make precisely such capricious gestures. Huddled together like two thin, blond beasts against the chill, the suggestion of salt harbored in the air between the tall buildings, she and Varnas turned south down Broad Street. To the East, rain hung in graphite and ashes over the Brooklyn Bridge. Osman Raffi was glad of the coat. He thought about the time he had shot a man and his brains had spat out after the slug in a crimson screw.

CHAPTER SEVENTEEN

LONG BEFORE THE WAR, her father had taken her to the Museum of Natural History, and she had pressed her face close to the cases of the Lepidoptera, her nervous breath misting the glass—thousands of wings, fixed open, pinned to pristine white canvas. An hour before, she had stood beneath the fossilized bones of dinosaurs, their aggressive skeletons held on wires and struts, the fleshless, bleached monsters arcing over her. Yet, looking into their empty jaws, counting the thorny teeth, she had experienced nothing of the horror she felt staring at the linen boards of that multitude of pinned moths, those neat and detailed rows of crucifixions, tiny Christs with delicately marked and dusty wings, stilled at last. A pollen of nausea had passed through her like a fluttering drift of decay, and she set one hand to preventing the bitter lurch of her throat. Then, her father's firm hand was on her shoulder. He had sensed her disgust and refused it. She would face it, again. He turned her face back to the case. It seemed to Campbell that in such a constellation of darkness, the only thing was to understand the background, the shroud to which the moths were fixed like the stains of a single, vast corpse, to discover its negative. The hand upon her shoulder was firm, but warm and reassuring, as though she had just been given an important gift—all that was required of her was to learn gratitude.

Now with Varnas, Campbell guided their walk to Battery Park. Beneath the trees, the unkempt grass fanned toward the green water, the promontory low against the press of the Atlantic. A chill came off the water and morbid clouds churned over Ellis and Liberty. Close to the path, a figure was wrapped in a drab woolen blanket like a chrysalis, dark eyes watching as they passed, a spittle of resentment glistening at their heels. There were several others sleeping or staring wretchedly from the lawn or slumped like straw-filled mannequins bayonetted against the bark of trees. Varnas smelled diesel and salt water. Pointing at the curved brick of the fort near the water, Campbell told Varnas how her father used to take her to the aquarium there.

"We would look into the pools and name the colors of the fish," she said. "There was a place with Japanese carp, and the bottom of the tank was a blue and white mosaic. People would drop pennies into it and make wishes. It really was very beautiful, with the large fish, orange and white, and the thousands of small blue tiles, and the golden light that reflected off the clean money. Don't lean too far, he'd say. I suppose he was thinking about my mother. Or, he might not have been. I imagine that they scooped up all the pennies immediately as the stock market failed."

Since the anniversary of his death, Campbell's father had tolled in her like the bell of a sunken boat, slow and deep in the current, reverberating beneath a fathomless weight. "But that isn't why I wanted to bring you here. I wanted you to see something." They found a bench where they could see the desolate promenade and the foaming edge of the water cast up over the wall. Lightning broke through the clouds like a crack in ice, but it did not rain.

Varnas was quiet. He put his arm around her shoulder and kissed her golden hair. She was shivering.

"It might take time," she said, and he told her that he was prepared to be patient. She apologized. "I know it's terribly cold."

He thought briefly of the man cocooned in the drab blanket,

straining in the grass—with hatred, was it? Yes, he thought, hatred could set one free. Had he seen some awful reflection or projection of hope in those black eyes?

They were silent for some time while the breeze came in off the ocean. Suddenly, Campbell stirred as if waking from a light sleep against his ribs. "There! There, look!"

Varnas stared. At first, he saw nothing, but a matted knot of filth mounted on a thin stick like a misshapen head. It was only when it turned slightly and stood in profile that he recognized it as a bird. "My God, is that a heron?"

"Yes, didn't I tell you? Look at it, Charles. Watch."

Campbell sat up straight on the bench.

He had seen seasick birds with oil in their fathers, ravens and pigeons picking along death's ragged edge with their deformed feet, but this was different. The heron appeared almost rotted through. With a grotesque arrogance, it stood motionless on the promenade beyond the lawn, its reedy legs, curved throat, and long beak forming a dislocated hieroglyph against the darkening horizon. Varnas' eyes had deceived him. They were further from the promenade than he had realized. He understood with a jolt of adrenaline that the heron was much larger than he had taken it for. "It must be—" It opened its wings, calling the air into its sickly plumage.

"Approaching six feet tall," Campbell said. "The wings are about nine."

"That's impossible!"

"No, it's right. Look at it, Charles."

With a sickening dread, he watched a young couple walking with a child of about four or five years old, approaching the monstrous bird on the promenade. They were dressed in raincoats and had come from the aquarium, immersed in pleasant conversation, not looking ahead, attentive only to each other. Varnas pushed himself from the bench, and almost cried out. Yet, when he blinked, the awful heron turned and hauled itself over the white-capped water, over an arc of spray from the waves slapping the sea wall. It went low, like a dirty shadow over the swell. Varnas' heart was beating fiercely. A heron of that size was so improbable that he could barely understand what he had witnessed.

Campbell said, "It's getting worse. That's the nastiest one I've seen yet. Solitary, not in flocks. They've all had that grizzly, necrotic attitude, but the others before were smaller. There's no damn habitat for a creature like that here. But now you've seen one, too."

Varnas was silent. He was lost in shock.

"After I began to notice them," Campbell said, "I checked at the library and the museum. There's a species in the mangroves of sub-Saharan Africa that is sometimes large enough to have a six-foot span, maybe seven, but this—" Campbell's weird laughter pressed gently at the membrane of hysteria.

Varnas was staring at the voided space where the heron had been, his voice diminished from shock and searching. The horizon was empty, save for a depression of clouds. "I don't understand."

It began to rain. Through the mist of it, Varnas watched people hurrying from the park, opening umbrellas, or covering their heads with scarves and folded newspapers. As he and Campbell rushed for cover, he searched for the vagrant cocooned in his blanket, but he was gone. Soon, the park was deserted. Thunder rolled above them. The black sky shattered with lightning, probing for the metal spires and peaks of the city. On Broadway, Varnas managed to flag down a cab, a Ford with a cloth roof that permitted some rainwater to blow in at the sides, but he told himself that it was better than nothing. They were, however, soaked through. Campbell didn't care that her shirt was transparent. Taking his freezing hand, through the static noise of the downpour coming off the asphalt and the drumming of the torrent on the slack roof, he heard Campbell call out "We can't outrun it!"

The cabman was lean and bald. His driving cap was one size too small, and as the rain found its way to him, the leather rim pinched and chaffed above his ears and at the back of his head, leaving reddened patches of scalp. He wore a navy rubber cape from which his hands extended to the steering wheel. The asphalt dragged in the storm. At Canal Street a horse had broken from its cart, and men struggled with harness and flapping tarpaulin. Beyond that, a taxi had broken down and blocked part of the street. The cabman idled patiently. "Don't worry," he said, "we'll get you home."

Varnas said it was fine. It was pleasant to be ferried through the city, even at an ebbing speed. From the subtle elevation of the cab, they could observe thousands of men and women pressing together without speaking. The rain was thinning now, and the city steamed as the blanched afternoon sun found stone and glass and magnified. Their clothes were still wet.

As they drew nearer to Varnas' home, the cabman half-turned in his seat. "Funny—You can smell the smoke from the Park, even with the rain. I remember throwing water on a campfire and how it would hiss and smoke and smell that way."

Campbell insisted that they get dropped off and visit the shanties, knowing already what they would find there. The smoke was weaker, but unmistakable as they approached. The shanties had been burned to the ground. The Central Park Hooverville had been reduced to a shallow black heap, and now to a shrouded gray paste in the rain. "Wolfowitz." Campbell did not see him among the small crowd of people who stood there. Varnas said that the only people he could see appeared to be cops.

One of the policemen, in plain clothes, saw two figures advancing across the grass, a man and a woman, both blond, neither dressed for the weather. He unfastened his brown raincoat and the badge at his belt flared brassily in the emerging sunlight. A tall, slim man in his fifties, dark hair streaked with white as he shook and replaced his hat, he moved toward them so that they met a few yards from the end of the row of steaming ash, where Wolfowitz's shack had been.

"I'm Kennedy." He extended his hand and Varnas shook it. Kennedy took a notebook from the pocket of his raincoat and flipped to a page of pencil shorthand.

"Dan Smith," Varnas said. "This is my sister, Jane."

Kennedy did not write the names in his notes.

Varnas understood immediately that the detective had not been distracted by such a weak deception. He felt Kennedy's eyes, like undersized garnets between his heavy lids, scrutinize him. Damn it, he thought, feeling his face stiffen against his will.

Kennedy said, "Not many people paid attention to this place before it burned. Now, everyone wants a peek. Do you live around here?" Kennedy's mouth was narrow and sardonic as he turned toward the scorched turf.

"We were just curious," Campbell said. "We smelled the smoke."

"The man who drove our cab told us about the fire."

Campbell waited, watching with cautious disinterest. After some moments, she asked, "Did you find anyone, say, in the place on the end—this one?" Her face was turned away from it, imagining scorched bones.

"This place was new. It came up suddenly. But the entire camp emptied out pretty fast when the fire took it, and there was nothing to salvage. No one stuck around to talk about it. It was probably an accident. Cold morning. The most likely explanation is that someone's fire got out of hand," the detective said. "And I bet the place was mostly empty anyhow, with these people out panhandling and scavenging, you see?"

"Oh, thank goodness," Campbell said. Still, she could not look. She was being careless, and she knew it, without understanding her motives.

Kennedy paused, scratched at an itch where his stubble had broken. "But there was one body inside. Burned beyond recognition. Likely where the fire started, yeah, in this one."

Campbell would not look. Varnas embraced her and averted his attention also. Unconsciously, he pictured the sheep that the analyst had killed.

Kennedy extended his right foot and pointed at the remains of Wolfowitz's shack with the tip of his brogue. "Poor bastard."

Campbell felt her shoulders trembling, a sickness swelling in her stomach. She coughed once and stepped back.

"But come here and take a look at this. Do you know what this is?" Heaped on the lawn were Varnas' coat and the plague mask.

Varnas shook his head.

Kennedy continued. "Strange, isn't it? Looks like a Hallowe'en costume to me, but why is it here, and why wasn't it burned up like everything else? Or is it chance? Someone shrugged it off last night as they went home, maybe?"

"That is unusual," Varnas said. "I don't think I could manage in your line of work. Mysteries—It's not like the radio."

"Yeah, right," Kennedy agreed. "It's like someone reads too many magazines, you know? There are some possibilities—and I'm telling you this, out of line, I suppose, because I doubt that we'll figure this out, and frankly, this scene isn't where the precinct is going to assign any manpower after this afternoon—Let's say this was arson, an attack on these people—"

"In broad daylight," Varnas offered.

"In broad daylight," Kennedy said. "That would be audacious—reckless—wouldn't you think? But you could say, maybe, either the deceased from this one hut had attended a party, which, given his status as a Hooverville resident seems unlikely—And why save his costume and not his own sorry skin? Or maybe the arsonist, or the killer left it for a reason."

"If it wasn't an accident," Varnas said.

Kennedy repeated Varnas' words.

CHAPTER EIGHTEEN

AMONG THE LOW DUNES, when Varnas had looked at his silver pocket watch, it had been four in the morning. The watch face shone like a nub of bone under crawling insect hands. Campbell regarded the stark monochrome blue-black of the sand scalloping the horizon. Her eyes had become accustomed to the desert moonlight and the deep distances. She was attired in sleek leather boots, jodhpurs, and a khaki shirt, and had brought her hip flask of cognac. Together, they sipped from it against the chill of the night. Certainly, it was dangerous for them to have walked out of the scattered lights of the Cairo suburbs to this place of darkness, out beyond the sound of barking dogs and dissonant radios. But now, that other Nile gassed and glittered above them in one silent arc of starry spine. There were more stars in that bisecting rim than Varnas or Campbell had ever seen, and it seemed to pull from its unfathomed distance at the surface of the silted river and its tumid banks with a vast phosphorescent ache. Campbell remarked that it looked like fur.

Varnas led her to the broken face of the Sphinx, the angles of the Pyramid of Chefren sloping beyond its rough haunches. Even at that violet hour, delineated by those assuming stars and the rime of the moon, the creature's head projected awkwardly, exaggerated from the leonine stone. The Sphinx's prosthetic face, staring smooth-eyed from its headcloth, was caged in wooden scaffolding as though an operation was being performed. Varnas felt for the perimeter ropes that by day kept the tourists back. Passing beneath them, they struggled down over abstract masonry, rubble, and slipways of dust, into the cool excavation precinct where the massive paws spread in sleep. Campbell thought it was all a wonderful blasphemy to trespass there. Watchful, Varnas whispered that they should remain still for a while, to become part of the blue silence, and stay alert to any sound of other footfalls.

There was a light breeze, colder than one might expect, he observed. Letting slack the tension in his flesh, now he perceived only a motorcycle rasping in the distance, to the west. He took Campbell's hand and led her along the Sphinx's flanks. She trailed her fingers across the coarse, chimerical surface, picturing her hand slipping into the creature's golden pelt. How must it be to caress a real lion, she wondered, and how different the living animal from the rigid dead in their sockets of limestone. When they returned to the point where they had started, Campbell whispered, "Tomorrow—"

Standing between the paws, Varnas lowered his head, and felt her dusty fingers in his dark hair, like talons on his scalp. Blindly, he reached for her shirt, opened it, and kissed her. She unfastened his trousers, taking the heat of him in her hand, pulling him, glistening into the golden place of her need. Standing with her riding pants tangled at the top of her boots, she could not open her legs very well, but he found her and pressed into her with the straining of a man at the limits of life, both of them lost in the riddle of it. Silently, they fell into the pulse. The stars blurred. Campbell, her body coming in elongated fluttering and pearlescent ripples, glimpsed the blank, scaffolded face of the Sphinx hanging over her in the night. Varnas looked upward, also, his mouth open, as though he could cry out, an exquisite loosening and tightening rising from his calves and into his sex until at last they were still and streaming together, pushing himself onto his toes as he had been in Venice under the dome, imagining the falling away of the earth.

Osman Raffi despised them. Not for what they did then, but for what they would do. He had followed them through the bare-bulbed and scented suburbs to the Sphinx. He had watched them descend, and had crawled after them under the rope line, pressing himself into that indignity of dust—

Now, it was the glassy November afternoon after the deluge when Raffi followed them to the Chrysler Building, that place he could not enter, above the city where he had not been invited, and where his countenance would not be admitted. For now, he remained, an ascetic presence in the amber block of the lobby. The plague coat which Raffi had worn in the rain was too hot now, and he placed it casually upon the tan chair beside the one he occupied. He considered how he might later pretend to forget it, and it occurred to him that it would be amusing if one of Detective Kennedy's people were to chance upon it there. But, that kind of distraction was of no great importance to him now. He got up to stretch his legs, fingering an unlit cigar, and regarding with contempt the lobby's stylized Egyptian motifs, the inlaid palm leaves, the fanning papyrus, and the dark polished marble. Even and especially in collapse, he thought, there was genuine obscenity here in America. He set himself within a vision of the city aflame, watching this great tower of the automobile magnate engulfed. As the doors opened, he spied into the elevator and imagined the high and depraved place it had taken Varnas and Campbell. In truth, he had no desire to experience it. It was merely that he resented this blind spot of the city where he could not follow them, of all the places he had watched them waste their time.

Years ago, during his time disguised as a colonel in the Egyptian Expeditionary Force, he had—he supposed—played some indirect, unconscious role in creating and sustaining places like this. Then, it had been better to side against the Turks and the Germans, swallowing and shaking his antipathy toward the British like an expedient drug. Strange alliances, he shrugged. So, it was. That was a mere moment of compromise in an uncompromising life, when he thought about it. Raffi combed his hair and smoked his corona. Restlessly, he returned to his chair and spent the length of his smoke seated, his legs crossed neatly, watching men in expensive suits entering the elevator doors, guillotining upward into the gleaming spire with its quartet of metal birds. At the last minute, he decided that he needed the coat. He got up and left, looking for a taxi.

"Why do I feel—" Campbell opened, searching for the right words, "that this is the last time we'll ever come here?" Before returning to the Chrysler and the Cloud Club, Campbell and Varnas had been to his apartment and had changed clothes. She wore no cosmetics that day, to get inside. Her hair was scraped back and severe, and she had dressed in an oversized—because it did not belong to her—glen plaid suit. Varnas wore his herringbone sports coat over a cream shirt, and gabardine trousers. He had combed his blond hair like hers.

She regarded the other tables, the mural of the futurist city in the clouds, the well-dressed men bent over their lunch, with no little sorrow. Varnas was looking out of the window. Patiently, she said, "I say, did you hear anything I said?"

"I think I was agreeing with you," he said. Leaning his ribs against the table in the act of lighting another cigarette, he whispered, "Do you really think that Wolfowitz was murdered? And that it has something to do with us?"

"I don't know."

"Why Wolfowitz?"

The waiter who arrived at their table was the red-haired young man who had attended them at Konigsberg's party. Varnas wondered if he would know them. The young man made an insinuating nod toward the water carafe, and Campbell winked at him. He would return with gin.

"I couldn't say. It's insane. The city is insane and all its occupants." She hated herself for the sense of relief she experienced, understanding that all the things she had ever confessed to the analyst had perished with him, burned down inside his brain. Did he have to die? These things flickered against her awareness, and for an instant, she was back at the gravesite of her father, despising him in his demonic aspect. "Anyway, Wolfowitz had a lot of clients. It might not have anything to do with me or you."

"But the mask and my coat," Varnas insisted, "left there like that. Was yours in the fire? I don't know, Campbell. It feels wrong, as though someone is trying to frame me."

"But you didn't really know him."

"Except that he probably knew me intimately through what you might have said on his damned couch." Varnas bristled. "Seriously, what did you tell him in those sessions?" Varnas regretted his words even as he spoke them. "God, I'm sorry. I didn't mean that, Campbell. It's none of my bloody business. Forgive me." He wanted to reach for her hands but could not do so without betraying her.

"What could I tell him, Charles?" Her eyes were fierce.

"I'm sorry, Campbell."

"Perhaps this was someone's intent, to slip a shadow of doubt between you and I, to have one of us crack." A moment later, the young man brought the carafe and set it between them. Campbell brightened. In her mannish voice, she said, "Ah, my crystal ball." She thanked the young man and ordered lamb loaf for them both. Pouring the gin, she said, "Now, let's see what we can see in here."

"My paranoia, I'll bet." Varnas smiled in self-deprecation. "Damn, the rain has come back. We're almost never without it." The tall window beaded above the hollows of the city. There was little he could do about the thorn in him now. The scar beside his eye pulsed. He was uneasy, haunted. Varnas drank quickly, burning his insides, pouring another glass—and this diamond clarity of gin and glass and sheets of rain set a vertigo in him that was not unpleasant—No, he thought, it was mystical, pushing into these narrow glassy hips and losing himself in delirium—he shook himself. If he had killed a man, then Campbell had approved of it. Who had decided it? It was not an accident, or else why take a shaving razor into the desert, if not to cut one's own throat? Yet, the corpse he had left in the sands of Giza those five years ago would not reveal itself to him. It was like a partially recollected dream, trapped behind a screen. Some mechanism of psyche protected him from final knowledge, so that he could not betray himself. He thought of Planet X, now named Pluto, coming into the solar system like the head of a storm of ice. What did it screen? Varnas lingered at the rim of his panic. Campbell's voice broke in.

"What are you thinking about?"

He hesitated, not wanting to sound mad. "My ghost, I suppose."

"Oh, I thought we exorcised all that the last time we were up here." She knew otherwise from walking with him in the street where he had wept beside the newsstands.

"I'm not so sure now. Maybe I am cracking. This morning, outside Battery Park, when you said we can't outrun it, what did you mean?" He was agitated, but managed to lower his voice, and leaned closer over the white tablecloth so that he could speak in a stage whisper against the noise of the club. "Look, I have wanted to kill more than one person in my life, and I don't know precisely what I did."

"Well, it's better that way, Charles. Really, it is."

"But it's okay for you to know? How can you live like that?"

"Live like what? Who says I live like anything? You wanted to do it, Charles. That's what matters to me."

"I just want—" Then, he did not know what to say. The guillotine had come down in him. He paused. "I think I might only be happy when I'm drinking. Jesus, the whole world's depressed." Contemplating his empty glass, before reaching for the carafe of gin, he summed it up. "It takes away—briefly—that haunted feeling. It takes all the death away. That's the exorcism. And I feel younger, rich with possibility and all the time in the world, not the slouching too, too solid figure I feel when the ghost is around—"

"Our ghost, Charles. It's *our* ghost." Campbell said.

"Well," he said, bitterly, "you weren't there."

"You can't absolve me from it, Charles. We agreed."

The urge to reach inside his unconscious and to pierce the membrane, to break the screen that protected him was indecent, dangerous. It took all of her will to prevent herself from doing it. She had resisted it, and she must resist it. He must break it down himself.

The red-haired young man brought their food. His presence at the table, slowly placing their plates, was almost sufficient to split the mood. Varnas was relieved, but worn down, his eyes pink from the alcohol and the acid press of his memories. He willed it all to stop.

When the waiter had gone, Campbell said, "Let's go back to my place, later. I'll change back. I can't keep on borrowing your clothes, or you'll have nothing decent left for yourself. Besides, you have no idea how exhausting it is being a man."

Varnas laughed. She was so immune. "We can wait out the rain, here, though," he said, and drank again.

Yes, Campbell thought, it was true that they would never return to this shimmering place of repose, this drunken rookery high in the Chrysler Building, this aluminum vault over the beaten streets. Yet, the rain did not stop, only gathered ferocity on the cold wind that bladed the bleak avenues. And what of her Egyptian detective? Could she even be certain that he existed, beyond the styled projections of her own guilt? Campbell could not eat. All she wanted was the quicksilver oblivion of the gin, and there was no little of that. God, she thought, I don't think this rain is ever going to let up. She swallowed again and wanted to croon with pleasure. And there was a version of her memory where, in the blue night, her detective was there with them in the spectral scaffolding that caged the Sphinx's face like bones. And against the ash of stars her eyes had met his while she and Varnas made love beneath him—Was she cracking up, also? It was too awful. The strain. The past would break through, eventually, she thought. It had always been merely a matter of time.

CHAPTER NINETEEN

As Varnas and Campbell were drinking, Osman Raffi used his skeleton key to open the door to Campbell's home. Although the stolen coat had kept much of the rain from his skin, the way he had been refused during the downpour by several taxi cabs served merely to enflame his resentment. Now, he stalked into the entry hall with a defiant arrogance, his weathered, handsome face concealing the hatred he felt in his bones. He switched on the lights and strode into the bohemian living room, noting the high ceiling and chandelier. Standing on the Egyptian carpet, he eyed the silk hanging like an open curtain at the edge of the mirror above the fireplace, the stalactites and stalagmites of pallid wax. From outside, the squall washed against the French doors to the small balcony. Strange, he thought, how the room felt familiar to him. Ignoring a worn and smoke-infused pack of tarot cards, he took the mono-grammed golf ball from the mantel and pocketed it, imagining some opportunity to return it to his employer. Removing the scarf from the mirror, he studied the serpentine ouroboros devouring and birthing herself around the antique glass. Raffi smiled at himself, baring his teeth as if to look for scraps of food between them, tilting his head in the light.

Over his shoulder, he saw the large bookcase. The delicate scent of old paper inspired him. Approaching it, he put his fingertips to the spines of several works on the occult, hermeticism, astrology, demonology—These accoutrements struck the Egyptian as pathetic. How long, he wondered, would he have to wait and amuse himself there? It would be better to have her alone and confront Varnas later. But one was rarely without the other. He would accept the circumstance presented when it came. Without deliberation, he slid one of the books from the shelf and examined it—*La Fisonomia dell'huomo et La Celeste*, published in Venice in the seventeenth century—leafing over detailed illustrations of the faces of men, animals, birds, signs of the zodiac. Indulging a bitter pleasure, he tore the first page from the book, then another. He peeled one of the illustrations out and began ripping the book apart in furious snatches. With that book obliterated, he removed another. With a gleaming shaving razor that he unfolded from his pocket, he destroyed the spine and scattered its leaves. He attacked the books as if they were flesh and blood. Raffi took a packet of matches from the mantel and lit a fire pile of coal and old books in the grate. Other volumes, he dragged to the floor and kicked until they disintegrated. Raffi removed his stolen coat, so that he could move more easily in his sweat.

He was furious now. In the bedroom, the Egyptian slashed Campbell's expensive pillows, cut deep and then gouged with his hands into the mattress where he envisioned her body, pulling the contents out with his fingers like a red sludge of her entrails. "Bitch," he said. "Bitch!" Pale feathers filled the room and stuck to the brilliantine of his hair and the wash of perspiration on his face. Spitting phlegm at the wallpaper, he paced to the kitchen trailing white down, and drank a glass of water. Smashing the glass in the sink, he took another and filled it. The swallowing left him breathless for a moment. His skull was filled with a swoon of sparks. He made several vicious incisions in the couch. The storm had accumulated in the streets, overwhelming the gutters, and forming frothing rivers at the curbside. In the living room, where the fireplace burned with books, he added more that he had scattered on the carpet. Panting, he threw open the tall windows to let in the edge of the rain and the cold air against his skin. Osman Raffi was the inheritor of a terrible vengeance, and he would have it here—

Campbell paid for the drinks and her untouched lamb. They negotiated their way between the tables and down the brass railed staircase to the papyrus designs of the elevator that would take them to Lexington Avenue. Varnas pressed for the lobby. As the aperture of the ochre doors narrowed, they looked out on the 66th floor for the last time. Varnas reached inside his jacket pocket. The leather notebook was there, under his fingers, the rubber band, and his pen, but something was wrong. "Damn it," he said, "I might have lost my news clipping." He took out the notebook and opened it. Where the original pencil record of the poems had faded, he had doubled the handwriting in ink. There was an ironic nostalgia in his voice. "Do you know, I've been carrying this for so long now that the poems that were copied into it—the stolen Hopkins poems— have been published? Isn't that something? I don't know why I carry it around, anymore." This twice-taken text, he thought, first in Knight's furtive pencil scrawl and now in his own ink tracing imitation of it, like a forgery. Knight, the pretender, he thought, the ambitious man who knows he must fail, that he is so, so mortal and envies the child. With care, he riffled the pages of the first half of the book. This form of divination, he put his faith in. The notebook, after all, had protected him from the Bedouin grenade that had taken his mother and father—

Man's mounting spirit in his bone-house, mean house, dwells—

He let the pages work, once more, and read aloud.

Not, I'll not, carrion comfort, Despair, not feast on thee;
Not untwist—slack they may be—these last strands of man
In me or most weary, cry I can no more. I can;
Can something, hope, wish day come, not choose not to be—

Campbell shrugged against him and asked what it meant to him. Now, it was Varnas' turn to recall the Sphinx, caged in its bone-house of scaffolding. He thought of a poor, trained falcon in its gyre, falling on the swindle of meat strung on a whirling thread. The falconer setting the string again and the bird returning to the air, only to plunge again. He thought of the untamed Christ—for there must be still some shred of Christian upbringing in him, at last, in the poems among all this paganism—breaking from his crossed flesh. He thought of Prometheus and his pecked-out long-licked liver, the towering bold ache of Babel, the pure desire to be, and poor priestly poet Hopkins—to be—to be—All of this he distilled in his mind but could not say simply. He and Campbell were reflected in the elevator mirror as he kissed her unmade lips. He wanted to say that the poem meant that he should have no despair of—nor toward—his dying, no mortal fear of death, but mad and inspirited with gin, he said nothing.

Even in the rain, the breadline at St. Francis of Assisi extended down West 31st Street and rounded the corner of Sixth Avenue, a brown, gray, smutted serpent of emaciated men in dripping threadbare coats and sag-brimmed hats. They shuffled, solemn and unshaven, along the sidewalk toward the tarpaulin where the friars tended the soup and damp loaves. The breadline reminded Detective Jerzy Kennedy of the war, photographs of the Eastern Front, of the mute-mouthed mud. In the bogs and black-branched hamlets of his ancestors, he might have expected such a line of men with their nerves and skin scraped thin by sudden hunger, but here in this great city, the sight of it retained the power to shock him. As he thought of the world, it struck him that the distance between the wastes, between all the famished and cratered spaces of the world had diminished, and he felt himself spiked with sorrow. Kennedy took out his police badge. He held it like an apology for passing along the line to the front without waiting and was depressed by the way so many of the hollow-eyed men shrank back from his authority. It was not the police badge like a relic from the old west, but the small silver cross he wore under his shirt that gave Kennedy comfort. He wanted to absolve the line of twisted men for whatever petty crimes they might have committed in their desperation, to reassure them that they were none of his business in this unyieldingly hard world. Yet, the detective sought first to absolve himself. At the front of the line, one of the friars in his brown frock recognized him and offered him a tin cup of broth. Rain splashed from the bald place on the friar's scalp as he held out the cup. Kennedy waved it away gently and apologetically, embarrassed that unlike the shivering rain-swept men all down the block, he really did not need it. He climbed the steps and passed under the portico.

Thank God, he had not missed the afternoon mass beneath the beautiful mosaic of Mary, bearing the wrapped Christ child on her shoulder and pressing the writhing dragon underfoot. He could almost feel the serene weight of her reassurance, her quiet dominion over death. Now, the tall candles were processed before the tight and coughing crowd. An elderly woman in a gray dress shifted on the pew beside him to make room. He removed his raincoat and his hat, pushing his fingers through the white streak in his black hair. Then he put his elbows on his knees and listened to the music of the mass. All that gold, all that glistering that is, he thought. Perhaps, that was also reassuring to people. There was the promise of something left. The congregants seemed content enough, washed over with some kind of grace and gratitude. Nonetheless, among the hundreds gathered there between the white columns, watching the white-draped altar, he was troubled. At the Agnus Dei, he found his eyes hot with the unfamiliar bulge of tears—*Agnus Dei, qui tollis peccata mundi, miserere nobis*—He had been disingenuous with the couple in Central Park, the ones he had encountered beside the damp ashes of the shanties. *Agnus Dei, qui tollis peccata mundi, miserere nobis*—He might have warned them of the dangers, but had chosen not to. He wondered if some fatal overconfidence in his own abilities to handle the case would lead to a greater disaster— *Agnus Dei, qui tollis peccata mundi, dona nobis pacem—*

When it was time to approach the altar, he was not certain that he should, but the crowd moved him forward. They smelled dirty, were poor and disheveled under the smoke of the censers, in the rippling wax, and the colored light issuing from the stained glass. And he was ashamed of himself. In his turn, Kennedy took the wine and the host on his tongue, consuming the blood and the body. There was an unfamiliar ambivalence in him, some failure. When the mass was over, although it was not the time to trouble anyone who might otherwise go outside to the breadline and give some solace, he sought out confession for himself.

Inside the wooden confessional booth, a single candle burned on a brass sconce. He was too tall to perch comfortably on the wooden stool. Pinched in, he was claustrophobic for a moment, then amused. He felt as he imagined the silver-suited men in the magazine stories might feel, flaming in their rockets toward the reel of stars. Jerzy Kennedy put his narrow sardonic mouth close to the trellised screen and spoke quietly. It had, he said, been only twenty-four hours since his last confession. The voice from the other side was an old man's voice, calm, and serious. He did not know the voice. No pushover, Kennedy judged. Through the screen, he caught a glimpse of crow's feet at dark eyes, a suggestion of olive in the skin. The detective continued. "I committed a sin of omission today, Father. I could have told the truth, fully, faith-fully, but I chose not to." He was quiet, then. The old Franciscan regarded the downcast green eyes of the detective in the webbing candlelight though the lattice.

"A venial sin, Jerzy, but I imagine—in your line of work—a peril."

Something about hearing his name spoken with such famil-iarity and understanding loosened the tension beneath his ribs. He went on. "The context included a man who—a dangerous man."

"You're in a position to stop him, are you not?"

"I think so."

The Franciscan spoke firmly. "Be certain."

"I mean, I am," Kennedy said.

"You have force of spirit, and force of law."

"Yes." Kennedy sat in silence.

"That's it?" The priest's voice was faintly dismissive and amused.

"Yes." Kennedy wondered if he really was worrying too much about it all.

"Make your prayer and you may go."

Kennedy did as he was required. He put on his coat and carried his hat. Outside, the breadline still plodded in pained inches under the rain. There must have been two thousand men there, he thought. He put his head down and walked through the downpour to Sixth Avenue. Flagging down a Model T radio car with his badge, Kennedy stepped onto the running board. "Kid," he said to the young patrolman, "My name's Kennedy. I need you to let me in and take me up town as fast as you can." Collapsing in the back seat under the loud thrumming of the canopy, the detective watched the wide waves cast by the car as the city continued to flood. The sky over the exposed girders of the Empire State Building was as menacing as Kennedy had ever seen it.

CHAPTER TWENTY

On Lexington, Campbell strode careless with gin into the slap of weather and stopped a cab, almost stepping from the curbside into its path. Varnas hastened after her and slammed the rear passenger door behind them. Campbell gave her address.

"I've never seen anything like this," the cabman said. "But I reckon I'll get you there."

From the back seat, they could barely see through the windshield. On the leather seat, in the smell of cigarettes and rain, Campbell and Varnas turned around to watch the Chrysler Building through the rear window, receding in the mist thrown from the street. Wind punched against the traffic. The flags outside Bloomingdale's were tangled on their poles. The figures in the avenue dripped like ink beyond the glass. They moved despondently, slow as limp flowers feeling their roots loosening in the eroding earth, resigned to the last slide of the soil. Everything was giving way. Campbell gave up watching. She leaned against Varnas, and he embraced her.

"In a few days," he said, "you won't need to go back to Venice. It'll be gondolas in Times Square." He checked his inside jacket pocket, finding the notebook quite dry under the tweed and its dark lining.

Campbell fumbled for a moment with her key. "Damn. Did I really leave my door unlocked? I must have, I suppose." She pushed it open. The entry light was on. Closing the door behind them, she whispered, "Hold on. I think something's wrong, Charles. I didn't do that." Automatically, she lifted her hand to the latch to lock it behind them, but he stopped her, shaking his head, no. Varnas put his hand on her shoulder and slipped past her. He could smell fresh smoke. Certainly, Campbell had not had a fire lit these last days of absence. Campbell felt her heart cramp, then break into a rapid beating. He told her to wait, and moved cautiously toward the living room, where he could see already that the lights were on. She heard him curse quietly, as though involuntarily, and followed against the stiffness of her anxiety. Varnas gestured that she should remain silent, and she covered her mouth with her hand.

Her home was in disarray. The floor was covered with the torn remnants of her books, thousands of pages ripped out, and spines and covers distorted as though they had been left at a busy intersection under traffic. Some seemed to have been thrown against the fireplace. It burned with a weak flame, as though it had been lit for some time, but was close to exhaustion. The tall windows were wide open, and rain had soaked the floor inside the balustrade. Campbell was afraid and wanted to weep. Her mirror had been shattered and lay with its shining serpent frame like a broken shield near the grate. The telephone line had been pulled from the wall, and the stem and earpiece destroyed. Sections of her wallpaper had been shredded from the plaster in white powder slashes. Struggling against quiet sobs of grief and anger, Campbell took up the brass poker from beside the fireplace.

Varnas picked his way over the fragmentary pages that obscured the rugs. It made it impossible to cross the room in silence, and he thought, that must be the point. There was a knot hanging in his guts, but the gin also set something cavalier in him toward an almost casual anticipation of violence, leaving him only barely agitated, and ready. Some of the scattered pages were wet and stained yellow with urine.

In the kitchen, Campbell discovered the basin of broken glass, her icebox ransacked. The sheer assault of it—The poker was heavy in her grip, the skin on her knuckles white with insult. Varnas was near the Chesterfield, staring at the wild surgery of cuts in the upholstery, tracing one with his index finger, the wadding projecting from the arms and seat cushions. Campbell touched his sleeve and inclined her head toward the rest of her suite. The rain must have come in heavily from the bathroom window and washed the short section of hallway that connected it to the living room. Varnas could see where the water had encroached there, also. Every lightbulb was burning, the incandescence like a scream.

At the same moment, Campbell and Varnas recognized one of the black leather coats they had worn for Hallowe'en and had left with Wolfowitz, lying on the floor. Campbell caught her breath. Varnas moved toward it, and beyond, into the hallway. When he reached the bathroom doorway, he glimpsed a polished monk strap shoe on the white tiles. A man stepped out from behind the shower curtain—

—Campbell knew the glistening midnight of his hair, the patient dusk of his complexion, the misshapen white of his smile, the penetrating eyes without their sunglasses. He was not tall, but he was lean and hostile in his tan suit, the jacket wet with his perspiration, unbuttoned over an untucked white shirt. Handsome and vicious, he appeared completely at ease with himself. She had seen him so many times, she thought. He had been following them through New York as he might have followed them in Cairo. To intimidate and to make her doubt herself, he had given something of himself away to her at Konigsberg's Hallowe'en party. She had seen him in her premonition of Wolfowitz's murder. She could not be certain that he had not been with them in the desert, in the scaffolded face of the Sphinx, in the souk, beneath the metal birdcage pavilions of the hotel, at the museum—had he been in Venice before that, on the ship, in Paris, at the Louvre? Feathers from her torn pillows clung to the damp angles of his face. They had settled on his shoulders and stuck to his hair. The shadow was before her now.

The Egyptian detective spoke in a relaxed tenor. "Good evening, Ms. Campbell. Mr. Varnas."

Charles Varnas knew him, also. He knew him from his childhood, in Cairo, when the Bedouin with the wide-set eyes had cast his grenade into his father's Suez Company office. He intuited also that he had been at Khaled's Place that night five years ago, after he had dropped the razor from the bridge into the Nile. Blocking the doorway, Varnas straightened. "What do you want?"

"Arrogant of the murderers to make demands," the Egyptian said.

"Who are you?"

"You know my name, Ms. Campbell."

"Osman Raffi—"

"The very same. It has been a long time."

"We're no killers," Varnas said.

Raffi grinned. "Come now, you've merely forgotten who you killed. That's all." Watching the twitch of the poker in Campbell's fist, dowsing for his blood, Osman Raffi took a revolver from his pocket.

"Be careful, Raffi," Varnas said, retreating a pace, back toward the living room.

The Egyptian looked from Varnas to Campbell and waved his gun casually. "Don't imagine that I won't blow the bitch's brains out."

"That's enough," Varnas said. "Here. You have us. Just tell us what you want. Campbell, put the poker down. Let's all remain calm."

She let it fall heavily among the destroyed pages of her books. There was a silence between them that seemed, to Campbell, to last a minute or more.

"But I remember you, Raffi," Varnas said. "Cairo, 1912. You were the one who bombed my father's office. I saw you from the window, running in the street." He saw his mother's dead eyes, the dust on her lips, the bleeding pits of shrapnel in her body. "You killed them."

Campbell wept quietly, glancing about like a frightened animal. Osman Raffi smiled. "If only that were true, Mr. Varnas."

Campbell whispered, "Stop, please. Please stop..."

Her Egyptian detective reached into his other pocket. "I have here," he said, waving something pale, "a letter from your mother and father, postmarked two weeks ago. They're very much alive, Mr. Varnas."

"That's impossible," Varnas said.

The voice was placid, insinuating. "I mean, this refutes—does it not?—your memory. You must see. I'm not your terrorist, Charles."

"He's a liar, Charles." Abruptly, Campbell had ceased weeping.

"Let's see," Raffi continued. "Indeed, what would the Devil's devil tell you?" He pretended that this search of his thoughts was arduous. "Hmm...Ah! Do you happen to know what a screen memory is, Charles? That's something like your problem." Raffi glanced at Campbell. "Campbell does. From our mutual acquaintance, Herr Wolfowitz, and has not Ms. Campbell listened to your excuses, patient and indulgent?"

"Shut up," Varnas said, unheeding of the revolver pointed at his heart.

"There's a kind of memory that conceals a more terrible memory behind it. Usually, it happens with childhood. But perhaps this neurosis is distorted in your case, or it may be that you are a very, very old child, eh? You've built delusions to limit your responsibility and your overdue remorse, to make you feel that bit—" Again, he pretended to search for the right word, "cleaner."

"Liar!" Campbell insisted. "Don't listen to him, Charles." The French windows clattered behind them, a pane exploding over the couch, and shards of glass chiming against the fireplace.

"Fabrications, Charles," Raffi explained. "Everything. All of it. You must know that the notebook has never protected you—"

He felt it there, shifting with his breath at his breast.

"There was never a schoolmaster named Knight. The poems in the notebook you think saved your life," Raffi laughed, "Oh God,

Charles. You merely copied them down at the library, just a matter of a few weeks, months ago. You did. Look again at the handwriting you've been tracing. It is your own. The past is breaking through, Charles, and the past is Hell. There was never any seduction by that man—You created him to assuage, to justify your crime in some most desperate manner. Poor tortured Charles Varnas, the orphan, running away, always running away. How can anything in this world be his fault?" Osman Raffi fanned himself with the envelope. "Charles—Please—Your artistry resides purely in your ability to deceive yourself. Are you sure you were ever really in Venice? My God, man, with her gifts and proclivities, you can't even tell if it isn't Campbell planting thoughts inside your head."

Campbell turned for a moment toward the fireplace—the postcard—before remembering that she had burned it.

"I remember," Varnas said.

"You think you do. But wouldn't you like to read this letter?" Osman Raffi continued to fan himself, lifting the revolver in his other hand, leveling it at Varnas' face, then Campbell's. Back and forth.

She knew the fingers that held the gun.

"I remember," Varnas insisted. "Everything I remember is real."

"Stop it," Campbell's voice was weak with sorrow.

The Egyptian said something else that Charles Varnas could not understand. He saw the lips moving, forming a perverse grimace, but heard nothing. Now, he was in Venice. Campbell had been asleep in their hotel room, and he stood on the balcony that overlooked the lagoon. Did not the black gondolas knock together in the tide? Yet, now he recalled the way Mr. Knight had held him down, the gray, snide schoolman's cruelty and manipulation, the pain in his childish innards, the faints of tea and Vaseline, and now this gorgeous, ambivalent girl—what was she to him?—his childhood returning—the vengeance of the boy that could not speak? The thoughts had come to him and oscillated against all his will, each image demanding its place. Briefly, he had stepped back into the room and groped around for an open bottle of wine, before returning to the dark overlook of the lagoon. Somebody was weeping in the next room. He could not have said if it was a man or a woman. Now, there was no moon. He had studied the stars for familiar constellations but found none.

"Do you hear me, murderer?" Osman Raffi demanded. "Do you hear me, also, you foul bitch?"

Campbell covered her face with her hands, slouching toward the bullet she knew must come soon.

The Egyptian spat, "Sir, I'm going to tell you the awful truth."

Campbell pressed her fingers tighter over her eyes. "No, no, no…" Whatever happened, she would not look.

In that moment, Charles Varnas saw it.

Between the ragged pages, in the carpet, soaked from the storm that had washed in through the bathroom window and flooded across the tiles, it was clear. Beside the place where Osman Raffi stood in the brightness of the lightbulbs, he saw a shallow but definite impression like a hieroglyphic, a strong line with three strong branches. Now, Charles Varnas smiled at the Egyptian. For, he knew it in the fearless and certain silence and lassitude that had come to him now, determined across an impossible gulf of time.

A heron's print—

PART FOUR

The destined lover, whom his stars
    More golden than the world of lights,
O'er passes bleak, o'er perilous bars
    Of rivers, lead, thro' storms and nights,

Or if he leave the West behind,
    Or father'd by the sunder's South,
Shall, when his star is zenith'd find
    Acceptance round his mistress' mouth:

—Gerard Manley Hopkins, from "The Lover's Stars"

CHAPTER TWENTY-ONE

THE HERON'S LONG BEAK penetrated Osman Raffi's back and erupted from his chest like a dripping golden lance. Transfixed, Charles Varnas could not move. He could only watch as the bird's tapering bill opened now, wide in its noiseless cackle, spreading its strong forceps of bone, the strange tongue livid in the awful pulse and jet burst of bright blood. It had broken through the Egyptian's shirtfront at the solar plexus, lifting him onto his toes, wrecking and raking upward like a mannequin on its long stiletto horn, the spike of some ancient gaff, as if a pair of closed scissors had passed through a thin sheet of paper making a narrow puncture, then opened wide, ripping effortlessly the pulp and pump of skin. It was like a marlin breaking the film of a blooded wave, raging mute in the spume and gargle of the Egyptian's death.

Varnas managed to glance at Campbell and saw that her hands were still shielding her face, her pale, beautiful boned shoulders heaving in terror. If he pulled her hands from her eyes—No, he could not. The revolver escaped Raffi's dead fingers and thudded upon the carpet. But the envelope was still pinched between his fingers when he hit the ground, among the thousand wet wings of paper that surrounded him. Slowly, the impaling beak withdrew from Osman Raffi's flesh, and he fell back on twisted knees, ghastly and lifeless, his mouth still open in an agony of disbelief.

Varnas shivered, caught between horror and admiration of the weird bird that stood executioner over the Egyptian's skewered corpse. It shook its feathers in the electric light of the bathroom. Raffi's dead eyes seemed to stare through the ceiling toward the blackness beyond.

The heron in Campbell's home stood more than six feet tall, the plumage of its folded wings the color of slate and smoke, its breast pale as a muslin shroud, uncanny strength in its yellow cane-like legs and the broad, brassy talons that had made their imprints in the wet carpet. The creature's powerful neck had the elegance of turned willow. It angled slightly sideways and curved its throat to show its black eye and to appraise Charles Varnas with cool detachment. Within its eye, Varnas saw a pinhole in the universe, and it took him in. A glimpse of galaxies—The heron's ancient heartbeat was in his ears, the ivory breast pulsing, the calm swaying stalk of neck shifting the bulb of its skull eerily, two thin feathers extending from the back of the head like antennae—Varnas was struck with the sense that Campbell had not seen several herons, but only this single prodigious bird passing through its sticky stations of growth. Magnificent now, and in that eye an underworld of reeded grasses and waving red plants, extending without end. Thousands of years—It had come to him, at last. The bend of the ribs suggested a soft coracle, a womb with an embryo, a downstream voyage. The wings, he thought, where he perceived the blue of the Nile amidst the gray, would surely span nine feet. These, the heron kept tightly folded like plates of intricate armoring. The lance of its beak still ran with gore. Varnas felt himself drop from its eye like a tear.

Without sound or ceremony, the apparition lifted one foot and stepped across the body of Osman Raffi, before picking its way— as though in some dislocated mangrove—through the paper that covered Campbell's floor. Varnas realized that Campbell had not yet moved, and that her trembling hands still covered her eyes. She appeared paralyzed. Turning away from her, he followed the heron. It began to move more quickly, still elegant and fearsome, parting its wings slightly in anticipation of flight. Varnas tried to run after it. Ahead of him, it made for the open French windows and lifted over the balustrade. Almost running through the litter of books, something compelled him to try to touch it, yet he could not—

Campbell lowered her hands and opened her eyes, revolving her shoulders and adjusting her place sufficiently to see Charles Varnas rushing, straining, arms outstretched toward the night. He struck violently against the rainswept balustrade, as though he did not know where he was. He made no sound. "No! No!" Campbell tried to cross the room after him, but it was too late. In horror, she saw his momentum throw his body off balance, tilting him from the balcony, sending him falling from the overhang toward the street. Against her will, she made for the windows to see, although everything in her refused it.

She was not yet across the room when she heard a loud beating at her front door that halted her like a statue. Nothing in her responded— The pounding at the door came again, and something in the red void of her nerves directed her toward it, glancing once at the open window and its ripped drapes, the missing pane of glass, the blackness of the rain and the nothingness into which Charles Varnas had plummeted. Before she reached the hallway, a scream broke from her. The door was opening. Campbell spoke to the shadow that stood there. "Help me—"

Kennedy told the patrolman to wait at the door, moving urgently into the hallway. "It's all right. It's okay." She had slumped to her knees in a sprawl of pages that, fleetingly, reminded him of folded birds. He pulled his Colt .38 from the holster at his ribs and crouched, speaking quietly and tersely, placing one hand on her shoulder. He whispered, "Are you alone? Who's here, anyone else?"

Campbell was unable to speak. She wanted to vomit.

"Okay," the detective said, rising to search her home, the barrel of his pistol preceding him. Instinctively, he made for the wing where Campbell's bedroom and bathroom were located. "Police! Show yourself and keep your hands where I can see them." Kennedy's voice was straight and impatient. "I said come out, you son of a bitch." It was better to go in assertive, he thought. He waited in silent agitation for several seconds before proceeding toward the hallway, and saw blood pooling on the tiles, soaking into the torn pages and the carpet where it met the bathroom. Presently, at the threshold, he discovered the stiffening, handsome corpse of Osman Raffi, rigorous, lying on its back. Close to the body, he saw the fireplace poker, gleaming in the red lagoon that the impaled flesh had made. The Egyptian had a look of amazement in his oval eyes. The mouth was twisted and filled with blood. There was a revolver on the floor. Kennedy put his gun away, removed his hat, and wiped the rainwater and sweat from his brow. Campbell was beside him now, wordless and pale as a blonde phantom. "You know this man?" he asked.

Campbell could not say anything.

"Okay. That's all right, now." Kennedy picked his way around the corpse, examining it and making small sounds of recognition and understanding from the fathoms of his detective reverie. The wet air that swilled through Campbell's place wilted the feathers that clung to Raffi's skin and hair. Campbell followed him into the bedroom and saw the razor slashes in her bed. "You're going to be okay, Ms. Campbell," he told her. "Sure, I know your name's not Smith, like Mr. Varnas said. But that deception doesn't matter to me. I'd do the same." Returning to the body, humming softly as he studied the poker, he traced an invisible constellation. "You were standing about here, when he attacked you, would you say?"

Something of Campbell's voice returned, thin with the static of a great distance. "I—I guess so."

"That's good. That's very good."

"But—"

"Here's what will happen. We are going to have to make a report, which means I'll have to obtain a statement from you. I'm sorry. I don't want you to have to live through it again. I wouldn't want to go through your memories if I could avoid it. But for better or worse, you're the sole witness to what happened here. I could at least take the statement here, but the truth is, your home is—" He waved at the state of things with his hat.

Campbell nodded, averting her eyes, as if she were guilty of some part in the destruction.

"We can get it cleaned up later, but it doesn't seem to me that you could or should try to stay here tonight. Do you have anywhere else, anyone who you could call?" He glanced at the destroyed telephone. "Or that we could contact on your behalf?"

There had been someone—

"We'll secure your windows, and people from the precinct will come here and look at the damage and see if they can learn anything. I don't want to get technical, but they'll, y'know—I can see this is very, very difficult, an awful shock." Kennedy spoke softly. "Okay, listen, this man was in your home. He was ransacking it, yes? That's when you came home and discovered him. He had a gun. You were afraid for your life. It was self-defense. Do you see? You're safe, now. You've never been safer. He's dead."

Then another voice cut in.

"Campbell! Jesus, Campbell! Are you all right?"

Kennedy saw her revived distress bloom in her green eyes like a flashbulb.

The voice, she knew as intimately as her own.

Campbell lost consciousness—

Charles Varnas had lain on his back, staring up into the illuminated rain, lit by the ornate buildings and the streetlamps with their curling iron necks. He had been dimly aware of the green wave of Central Park, the scent of its tendrils of grass, ivy, boughs, and weaving roots—And yet, he was not certain where he was, precisely. The breath had been beaten from his body, abandoning him to the needle pain of hollow lungs struggling and sucking at the watery sky, for any thin comfort in the turbid street. He had seemed to be suspended above it.

Varnas had tested his fingers, and they had moved. There was the feeling of dampness in his socks, and this he felt passing into his skin, and he felt it in his nerves with profound relief. He struggled to remember—Yes, Osman Raffi had been there with his revolver—Raffi was dead—He saw him slip from a golden lance— The heron's eye—It had come to him as a command from God— He recalled the uncanny speed with which the heron had crossed Campbell's apartment to the open windows, and how he had felt when he saw that it meant to leave—to leave him—some impossible loss in his throat, the infinite melancholy of its flight threatened to destroy him—if only he could touch it—catch hold of it and prove to himself that—Charles Varnas saw himself falling from Campbell's balcony—The heron's eye burning bright in the rain that came in dull stripes of mourning. Now, he felt the fastness of falling, once more, the grip of the earth. He saw the gray wings turning over him.

Slowly, in the mad recession of his pain, he had discovered that he was caught in the canopy of a police patrol car. Metal struts and torn fabric furled about his body like a dark flower. The folding roof must have broken his fall, he thought. The notebook—It was not there, not in his pocket, close to the place where his heart still beat in its tender cavity—Varnas began to laugh. The air was empty now of anything, save the wash of rain.

The deluge had cleared the evening street sufficiently, so that no one had seen his plunge, and no one was there to witness a man with peroxide hair disentangling himself from the imploded roof of a patrol car. When he stood on the flooded sidewalk, he was in pain, but found himself quite uninjured. And this was almost too much for his comprehension as he hastened back inside the Campbell mansion. As he would think of it later, Kennedy and the

young patrolman must have been ascending the stairs to Campbell's suite at the moment that he followed the heron out of the
window.

Varnas found the patrolman waiting at Campbell's open door.
"This is my home," he had said. "My wife—you have to let me in."
The lie was quick and sufficient to the moment. Without waiting
for acknowledgment, Varnas shrugged between the man and the
doorframe, and into the hallway and the living room. There, he
saw Campbell and the detective he recognized as Kennedy from
the ashes of the shanty town. Kennedy knelt in the drift of bloody
pages, having caught Campbell's unconscious fall.

"Help me, Varnas," he said. "Let's get her to the couch."

"There's brandy in the kitchen, if Raffi didn't smash everything." Varnas took Campbell while Kennedy searched the kitchen.

Returning with a small bottle, he said, "How did you know
Osman Raffi was here?"

Campbell shifted, her awareness returning just so that she
heard Varnas' voice saying that she had managed to call him.

"Where is he now?" Varnas asked.

"Back there. He's dead. She got him."

Varnas lifted her shoulders and gave her a sip of brandy. "Oh
God, Campbell—"

"Charles—You came back."

CHAPTER TWENTY-TWO

DETECTIVE KENNEDY LOOKED OUT over the balustrade at the water rising in the street, the patrol car too close to the building to see without leaning precipitously. He spoke rapidly. "Listen, Varnas, by the time I could get you both down to Centre Street, honestly, I think you might not get back up here again, with the rain. You live quite close, I know. What do they call it—a hundred-year flood? This is more like five hundred. I know it's awful, but is there any way that we might—talk here?" He inclined his head toward Campbell. "We could get a statement, and maybe you could retire to your place?"

"That would be for the best, I think, yes."

"Thanks. Someone will come for the body." Kennedy looked around the room. "I'm sorry about this, truly."

Campbell gained another thin plateau of consciousness and Varnas said, "Don't be alarmed. Detective Kennedy is going to get a statement, and we'll be able to get out of here presently."

She looked at him, disbelieving. Fragments of her perceptions were still clinging to the image of the Egyptian aiming his revolver at her face, and the grotesque—yet quite reasonable—idea that she was about to die with a hole in her skull. And yet, the greater number of these slivers and shards, like a smashed glass photo plate, captured a terrible blurred image of Charles Varnas going over the slick balcony to his death.

"That's right," Kennedy said. "It won't take long."

Something of her climbed back to the surface of things, and Campbell managed what was required. She recounted that she had returned home and discovered that an Egyptian named Osman Raffi had gained entry to her home. He was ransacking her possessions and did not hear her opening the front door. When she snatched up the telephone and called Varnas, the Egyptian had pulled his revolver and said he had come to kill her. She could not guess his motive. Fearing for her life, she ran the poker into his body. Kennedy took all of this down.

"You see, I've been following Osman Raffi for a year," the detective said. "You didn't know I was at Konigsberg's party, did you?" Although he was pleased with himself, he attempted to lighten the scene with self-deprecation. "Do you remember a particularly dashing vampire with a fancy reversible cape?" Kennedy grinned, "That was me."

"I do remember," Campbell said. "Now you say it, I can see that it was you."

"But look, I did something that I'm not proud of. I let you believe that Wolfowitz is dead when he isn't."

"He's not dead?" Campbell stared at Kennedy. Her green eyes were wide with confusion.

"No. In the park, when the shacks were burned, I told you there was a body, but that wasn't true. You didn't want to look at the ashes because you were afraid of what you'd see. So, I took advantage."

"Oh, God," she said, clasping her hands to her breast.

"And, you didn't know that Osman Raffi had been seeing Wolfowitz too." Kennedy rubbed his eyes with his knuckles, some pollutants in the rain stung them. "Raffi was a psychopath. He had told Wolfowitz that he was the Devil's emissary, a kind of Mephistopheles delusion. It was strange, though. Strange, because he did seem to know some things that, for the life of me, in God's name, I'm not sure how he knew them."

Campbell felt Kennedy shifting his attention from her, on the couch, to Varnas kneeling beside her, and then returning it to her, distressingly reminiscent of the way Raffi had shifted his revolver. She remembered the letter—

"But then," Kennedy went on, "I don't know what you told Wolfowitz, either Ms. Campbell. So, maybe he got some of it from extorting Wolfowitz. And I don't know, yet, how ethical the good Doctor Wolfowitz was under that kind of pressure. What I do know is that Raffi's obsessive behavior revolved around you and Charles Varnas, and visions of some kind of vengeance. For what, God knows. I've been watching you, also. All you do is drink. Back when Wolfowitz's office was in Chelsea, after his sessions, Osman Raffi would wait to catch a glimpse of you."

"Jesus, I never saw him there—Not once." Campbell shook her head, and glanced toward the corpse of her Egyptian detective, suddenly hollowed out in her home. His blood was everywhere.

"Anyway, we—the department—have taken care of Wolfowitz. He'll be okay."

From the ruined couch, Campbell leaned on her elbow. "Why was he so interested in me?"

"That's a mystery to me, but I might get something of his motivation from Wolfowitz. I've learned a lot from him already, and I hope to learn more, given time. Was he trying to blackmail you? What do you think is in the letter he's holding?"

"No. I don't know. But you don't believe all that Devil stuff."

"I think we both do, Ms. Campbell, in our different ways." Kennedy put his hat on, to signal that the interview was over. He made no other immediate move to leave. "I'm a Catholic. It's merely that you and I are on different sides of the coin."

"That's all?" Varnas said. He saw that Campbell had been about to say something and felt compelled to cut it off.

"I have everything I need. You'll take care of her, Mr. Varnas?"

"Of course."

"We'll stay here for the time it takes, to get an ambulance, and

follow to the morgue. My colleague can radio from the patrol car."
He looked around the room, again. "Well, I imagine you'll be able
to return in a few days, if you want to. It'll be completely secure.
Can you pack a few things without disturbing this, uh, this distur-
bance? You might yet catch one of the night's final cabs, out there,
if they haven't all drowned."

Campbell agreed.

"God go with you," Kennedy said.

Presently, they descended to the street, Varnas holding the
gray valise Campbell had assembled. The rain had ceased, at last,
and Kennedy was right. A solitary cab would wash toward them
in the vacant, moonlit street, moving stubbornly in the bitter cold
of the flood that had crested the sidewalks. The drains were silent,
too overwhelmed to sound with any flow of water. In the shroud
of her shock, Campbell did not notice the collapsed canopy of the
patrol car, but Varnas eyed it superstitiously as they drove away.
He wondered what Kennedy and his patrolman would make of
it. Inside the taxi, with its smell of cigarettes and damp decay,
they clasped their hands together. As the cab passed beneath the
streetlamps at the edge of Central Park, she regarded his unscathed
hands and face. He should be dead. They could not speak. Slowly,
the violence of Campbell's place receded like a nightmare too
abstract to recall, and with it the death of Osman Raffi.

Now that Campbell and Varnas were gone, Jerzy Kennedy
allowed himself some minutes to think. He prised the envelope
from between Raffi's fingers and held it up to the lightbulb in the
bathroom. He could tell that it was empty. If it was blackmail, it
was a bluff. He put it back before he summoned the patrolman
away from his vigil at the door. A psychopath—Wolfowitz was
right about that. Wolfowitz was an eerie character himself, with
that black-eyed James Joyce aspect. "Oh, Lord, I'm sorry, what's
your name, son?"

"Pete. Pete Johansen."

"Okay. I didn't mean to be rude by not asking. I guess I was a little frantic. You see why. How long have you been on the force, Pete?"

"Two years, give or take."

"Have you seen many dead bodies, Pete?"

"Some."

"Good, okay. Come here."

They stood over the body, the blood blackening and tacky, white feathers trapped in the surface. Raffi's dead eyes seemed to stare between the two men to a featureless space on the ceiling. Johansen knelt down, then rose and circled the corpse, keeping his shoes out of the slick. The smell of the grave was gathering at the mouth. To Kennedy, the patrolman appeared to be in his middle twenties. Of medium build, blue eyes, brown hair underneath his cap, Johansen's uniform steamed faintly as the rain evaporated from the cloth in the warm room.

Kennedy said, "Do me a favor. Examine the poker."

Johansen crouched again. With the backs of his thighs against his heels, his wet shoes creased sharply against his feet, so that he wanted to stand again almost immediately. He bit his lower lip and studied the scene for several seconds. "All right."

"Now, examine the fatal wound here."

This, Johansen did, also. Bent at the waist, before he had finished with his concentration, he anticipated Kennedy's next question.

"What's wrong with that wound, Pete?"

He spoke confidently. "Detective, it's from the back."

"We're looking at an exit wound, yes." Kennedy circled. "Does that matter to you?"

"Not if he was prowling around her bedroom with a gun."

"Look at the tip of the poker, again."

"It's pretty blunt."

"Too blunt? Let's say it's you with a heavy brass fireplace poker, and you're behind this intruder, and you can see his gun is out. Wouldn't you smash his skull with it?"

"Probably." Johansen drew a hand across the stubble that itched his face now. "I'd have the strength to, though. Maybe she could, but it's doubtful. She'd have to knock him cold first time, with him having a gun. That would be a hell of a blow for a nervous girl."

"Do you think that girl could run this man through with a blunt instrument like that?"

"Uh-uh. I don't think I could."

"So, what should we do with that, Pete?"

Johansen hesitated. He glanced at the corpse, at the gray-olive complexion. And he thought of the petrified and beautiful blonde whom the Egyptian would almost certainly have murdered, saw in his mind the close-range bullets blowing out of her back, the scorched pits in her breast. He pictured a shot to her pale brow, the wound blooming hideously. Nausea pulsed in his throat. "I don't know." He shrugged the images from his consciousness and was left only with contempt for the dead man. "Like you said, does it matter?"

"I don't know," Kennedy lamented. "Let's go down and radio the wagon."

When they reached the car, Johansen ran his fingers across the collapsed canopy, pooled with rain at the edges where it wasn't torn, its struts mangled and broken. "I'll be damned," he said. "People have it in for cops." He looked up and down the street. "The front looks all right, and so's the radio. We'll be able to drive fine, but we might have to hunch in a little."

"Call it in," Kennedy said. "And tell the wagon to step on it. The only people left out here are the fish." He wondered how long the breadline outside Saint Francis of Assisi had persevered through the storm. Abruptly, Kennedy realized that he had not crossed himself before the dead body, as was his custom, even with the worst of the dying and dead men he had witnessed—a small shock to his nerves, that felt like awakening to a lick of lightning and waiting for the weight of the thunderclap. It troubled

him as the ambulance arrived, and as the sheeted form of Osman
Raffi was removed. Like he's ready to be embalmed and mummified, Kennedy thought. The same sensation of hanging, suspended
between the revelation and its deciphering followed him as
Johansen drove him back down to headquarters, where the city
appeared to have been abandoned. What, he asked himself, had so
subtly tied his hands?

CHAPTER TWENTY-THREE

CHARLES VARNAS AND CAMPBELL reposed at the opposite ends of his couch, dressed in white cotton bathrobes, their eyes fixed to penetrate the mystery of the other, their knees drawn up in that imaginary gondola over the canals and lagoons of death that would come to New York in the night. He had made them each a large, cold martini to ward off the evils of the evening. In the golden candlelight that was also part of the spell, Varnas did not dare to ask what Campbell had seen. He had lain in the death nest that his fall had made of the patrol car roof. Had she seen anything of the great heron killing Osman Raffi? Had she witnessed him running and reaching after it with wild, empty fingers?

For her part, Campbell could not yet bring herself to ask why Varnas was not dead, how he had killed the Egyptian, and what weird malevolence had set him into that abyss of suicide. For Christ's sake, she cried inwardly, how had he returned from death? Could it be that his wild ideas about himself, his immortality, were correct? The rain hissed against the windows and Campbell was convinced that the city would drown. Now, she saw that Varnas' blue eyes were glassy with oncoming tears, and this riddled her with all the palsies and aches of an urgent, fresh grief. She watched Varnas drink, as if he was about to speak yet required that much more heat in his ghostly flesh. If she had not put her own cocktail glass against her trembling mouth, she might have cracked, for she sensed that Charles Varnas remembered—

He said, "Does the name Bennu mean anything to you?"

Campbell answered, "I've been asked that question before."

Yes, Varnas thought, and a distant smile came to him as he affirmed it in his mind—Yes—Yes—I have come out of the heron's death nest, and now, everything is—

"My father asked me that, once." The martini did its work. She experienced the descent of a calm, as though the transparency of alcohol was a thing that had detached from the chandelier and cool plaster ceiling and floated down over her like a shawl of star-pinned jelly. "Are we having that seance you wanted, now?" She smiled. Death, she understood, had been trying to speak through Charles Varnas for five years.

"I remembered everything, Campbell." He met her green eyes. "Everything."

"You know—"

"The Adversary."

"And how do you feel, now?"

"I think—" He scanned the room. "At peace."

"It's unexpected," Campbell said.

Varnas wondered, did he catch the intimation of a question? He answered, "Yes."

Campbell circled the question her father had put, and that Varnas echoed—Bennu—Of course, Rafferty Oran Campbell must have known what the grizzly sight of the herons massing in Lower Manhattan would provoke in her, in that wing of guilt where their crime against her father was concealed. The birds were something of her father's premonition, also. He suffered it, even as he derided it, knowing secretly that the tragedy was not one-sided. The heron in Battery Park was, perhaps, as much a reassurance as a warning. Then again, she thought, he might have been probing to see if she had been contacted. Had her father been afraid—afraid of her—when he came that night before Hallowe'en? She addressed

Varnas, again. "That morning, we had been at the necropolis, all the tomb world spread about us, sarcophagi lost like splinters in the immensity of it, and the men sifting through the sand—"

Varnas tilted his head and put a finger to his lips in recollection. The corpses—undisturbed for thousands of years—existing uninterrupted—seeing it all from the high depths of death—

Campbell continued. "We had spent some time at the museum. We had seen the papyrus with the beautiful heron standing in his woven gondola of reeds. And the hawk-head, Horus, with his eye—"

Varnas broke in. "I saw the heron, Campbell. It returned."

"At Battery Park."

"No. Again. It must have come in through from the balcony before we arrived, and it went out just so." Varnas sipped his martini.

Campbell understood him and was placid. She looked at the window in Varnas' living room. "You didn't kill Osman Raffi."

He shook his head. "But Raffi was your father's agent."

"His Mephistopheles."

"If you like. That's their arrangement."

Campbell waited.

In his reverie, Varnas thought of Mr. Knight, and his study with the crucifix on the wall. What the schoolmaster had seen, and sought for further in the boy Charles Varnas, he had misapprehended. Knight had mistaken that latent permanence of self for the immortality of poetry, some quiet talent in the boy that would outlive them both, and that he desired in the deepest catacombs of the stars. There must have been moments when Knight considered if it might all be projection on his part—the unkempt boy bent over his desk, the glamor of the gift diminished by approaching it. Now, he wondered what species of presence Knight had been. Was he anything like the detective, Kennedy, laboring toward the holy source, the grail, the fountainhead of each of their crimes? To his introspection came the image of the Adversary bleeding into the dune of five years past. Yet, Varnas was quiescent, certain, and like an innocent whom experience could not corrupt—This was the truth the heron gave—

"Charles, are you all right?" Campbell asked.

"I'm fine, yes. I really can see it."

He was silent for some time. When he spoke again, Varnas' voice was slow and deliberate. "Osman Raffi was right about the notebook, in one respect. It never has been a protection for me. I was wrong to have believed that. But it was, I suppose, more modest than the alternative—that my infinite survival required no magical object. I understood that when I found that it had slipped from my pocket and fallen straight though the death nest."

Campbell was confused.

"In a few hours, my notebook will be found on the floor beneath the back seat, under the ruined section of that patrolman's car—that's where I fell, into the roof of the car. I couldn't reach down inside to retrieve it. And I had to get back up to you, now that I had understood that the police must be at your door. They'll see Knight's inscription with my name. Kennedy will be back. Your father's very intelligent, Campbell."

Campbell muttered, "Jesus Christ—"

"Do you still have any of that cocaine you bought from the Chinese? I might want to remain awake and alert." Varnas half-turned from his place on the couch and lifted the Smith Corona from his side table.

"What are you planning to write?" Campbell said.

"Whatever comes through."

"Did you die—truly—when you went over the balustrade?"

"I don't know. Maybe it was luck, and just a coincidence that the patrol car was sitting there in the rain."

"But you don't believe that." Campbell recalled what she had said to Kennedy about devils.

"I know I'm not dead now that I'm here with you. No, I've been thinking about the heron I sketched in my notebook where the poems ended. I wonder about the interval between death and rebirth—Like the blink of an eye—quicker? It could be, that is all the time that elapses—one flicker of its retuning life in every five centuries."

Campbell was pensive, listening.

Varnas said, "What if we get up, look out of the window, and five hundred years have elapsed?"

The typewriter was in his lap, with the blank sheet of paper he had scrolled into it those weeks ago, on the day that something had conspired with the breeze of Lexington Avenue to get to him with the newsprint account of Falconer's lecture.

"Still, you managed to shut him out for five years," she countered, drinking. "As for intelligence, you must have noticed how easily cynicism is mistaken for intelligence, lately. My father desires merely to exact his revenge on you and me. You think that Raffi threw the bomb that killed your parents, preemptively? Was he really trying to kill you, back then, before we met? What happened?"

"No. I think that before your father took possession of him, the ordinary man in Osman Raffi really was against the Suez Company. When Raffi was under him, however, it became an experiment, of sorts. Your father wanted to be sure that I was what he suspected. It was one of his perverse ways of awakening me to it, in myself. It became a signal in my unconscious. And it was part of the conspiracy that brought us together. I can picture him scanning the world for a mate for you. We were designed to meet."

Campbell sighed. "Is this what madness is, Charles? Two people driven insane by remorse?"

"I can't feel remorse any longer. Do you?"

"No."

"I forgot myself after the Adversary. I might have succumbed to it. It was going to come down on me like—a mob of brilliant spiders. Campbell, we can't afford the guilt, the endless web of melancholy that he intends. It doesn't belong to us."

"I think it was Raffi who was on the beach with me when my father cast my mother's body into the ocean." From her gown pocket, Campbell tipped some of the cocaine from its tin onto the slope of her thumb and inhaled it. Varnas set the typewriter between them. She passed the tin to Varnas, and he did the same as she had. Moments later, the metal stalks of the machine began to slap against the page, the word C-O-N-F-E-S-S-I-O-N printing upon the ivory paper—

CHAPTER TWENTY-FOUR

JERZY KENNEDY WAS RELIEVED to be out of the rain, and out of his saturated suit. In his striped pajamas, he pulled his olive easy chair closer to the radiator, appreciating the velveteen upholstery where he would sit with his warm milk before retiring to his bed. In the kitchen, he lifted the pan from his hot plate and watched the steam of his camping cup. How pleasant it would be, he thought, to retire from detective work altogether, and to spend time traveling, driving up north to see Niagara Falls, the old adobe churches in the deserts of the southwest, the Meteor Crater, or Yosemite, and the Grand Canyon, and all of the wonders of the vast country. To go deeper, to go out—He thought about the breadlines. He thought about the suicides he'd heard about. And he said to himself, if only men could use their resources correctly, and it wasn't always money, and money, and more damned money.

He thought about the safe at Campbell's apartment. They had discovered it close to her bedside while searching for other evidence. Raffi didn't have any significant amount of money on him. Perhaps he was hoping to find it, after killing Campbell. As they tooled the mechanism, the anticipation of a fortune had glowed in Johansen's eyes. When Kennedy opened it, the safe was empty. Campbell was broke. Whatever she had used to sustain herself, it was gone. He imagined an hourglass with a heap of sand stopped dead in the lower bell. Everything seemed to have run out for Campbell and Varnas at the same time, he thought.

Kennedy was exhausted. He understood that it was making him irritable. The scale of his drab apartment, considered against the place he had been, made for an awkward comparison. Even with a dead body lying around, there was more room at the girl's place. His mouth settled into its sardonic smile. He would have to atone for that thought. He finished his milk, and washed the cup in the empty sink, always putting things back where they had come from. At last, he made it to his bed and his heavy woolen blankets, where he lapsed into a swift and dreamless sleep.

There was a presence. Something spectral reached into the fathoms of Kennedy's slumber and warned him that he was not alone. Campbell? He kept his eyes closed, but he felt it—the nerve-chilling vertigo that came with that certain awareness that someone was standing over him. It was almost childish. Cautiously, the detective moved his right hand beneath the blankets across his chest to find the silver cross on its chain about his neck. Against his will, he opened his eyes with the first sound of the other's voice.

"It's all right, Kennedy."

The room was dark, but the ambient light of the city through the open, moth-eaten curtains partially illuminated the shape of a figure—a tall, deep-chested figure looming over him like a coroner at a corpse. Kennedy gasped, drawing back against the mattress. "What do you want?"

The other spoke softly, with an accent. "You know my daughter, the murderess and her mate."

"What?" Kennedy struggled to steady his breathing.

"My name is Rafferty Oran Campbell."

"Campbell? I don't understand."

"I'm the girl's father."

"But yes—only this evening—I really only met her this evening."

This man, Kennedy told himself, could not be her notorious father.

That man had been dead for a year. Kennedy pictured his gun in its holster, hanging from the nail on the back of the kitchen door where his suit dripped onto the floral print linoleum. He said, "I'm going to reach with my left hand and turn on the bedside lamp, nothing funny." He kept the cross in his right hand.

"Do what you will," the Adversary said.

Kennedy, supporting himself with one elbow, saw the intruder plainly now. He had settled into the green chair beside the radiator. Like Kennedy, he seemed to be in his fifties, dressed in a coal dust suit. His hair was black as tar, and his eyes the same vivid green as the girl's. The detective observed a deep sorrow in the man's face, the furrows in the brow that contracted into a pale steeple of despair. The apartment was filled with the sickly, putrescent odor of death. Kennedy perched on the edge of his mattress in his striped pajamas. The spectral feeling of vertigo was still in his flesh. "Oh, I think I know who you are." He gripped the crucifix tighter, and it bit into his lifeline drawing a bead of bright blood. "Agnus Dei—"

"Poor Raffi—"

"The Egyptian was important to you. Why? Who was he?"

"You have doubts? That's disappointing in a religious man. He was my trusted emissary, my man in the cities. Raffi was precisely as he told Wolfowitz, the Devil's devil."

"Wolfowitz—" The malevolent and penetrating stench of the Adversary was in Kennedy's face.

"Wolfowitz is dead."

"God—"

"Look at me when I'm speaking, Kennedy. I'll razor the fucking eyelids off your idiot face, so I bloody will!"

"I'm sorry—I'm sorry, but I'm very afraid of you."

"You thought I was dead. I merely left the scene for a while. That's a mistake Varnas and my daughter made, also."

Kennedy forced himself to stare at the presence in his room. He wished that he could lose consciousness, that his heart would split, or some lightning of his nerves would stroke across his brain. He was ashamed, but in that moment, he desired more than anything to die immediately of his own accord, to be removed by his faith. But it was all impossible.

"That bitch and her moth betrayed me. They killed Raffi, yes, but they took something else from me. But you have your doubts. I can see that. You suppose I might not be real."

Kennedy suppressed a gag reflex. "No, no doubts. I might not have believed it, but now I see you, here in front of me. It's undeniable—You, at least, are real." Kennedy tried to catch his words, but they were out. Yes, he doubted. But there was nowhere else to go. He must go on. He did not know what he would say next. "I don't know what they took from you. It's not my concern. But I think you want to lend me some share of your pain. I can endure it." There—there it is! he thought. Like the antidote to a venom, Kennedy recognized the wash of courageous fidelity streaming again within his flesh, grace entering him in a starry torrent of consolation. It would be all right, he thought. "But Devil, I will not hear you."

"What did you say?"

"I say damn you, Rafferty Oran Campbell, or whatever you are! In the name of God, damn you back to your Pandemonium."

The Adversary laughed and showed Kennedy the gun he had taken from the detective's holster in the kitchen. The stench as he opened his jacket was overwhelming. "It's funny,' he said. "Everyone knew about my death, but no one actually witnessed it. I have been indulged well by the passage of time. If you can buy life after death, one can surely buy death itself more cheaply. Or its appearance—smashed meat, some broken bones, a bucket of blood, and an empty suit. Who would even want to look after a fall supposed to be from that height? Perhaps I paid off a rookie cop named Johansen."

"You're lying."

"How else should I explain my presence?"

"I know what you are."

"And in that part of 1929, on that side of the 24th, almost anyone could afford a headstone. Just you fucking prove that I jumped, you pederast! You shit-faced pious prick, you. Do I smell something here? Is that you? Don't be afraid. Be advised, you know that I think Campbell's completely fucking monstrously insane, but she could talk Charles Varnas into anything with her platinum cunt. Keep that in mind. Oh, I tried to prevent it, but they ran, ran, ran…Passing out of this world that's preoccupied with merely existing, with base being, with subsistence—Well, that's easy, Kennedy. Even you've considered it, yes?"

Kennedy said, "I'm not special."

"Correct. And all of this is all outside of your jurisdiction, even as a matter of the soul. Imagine this, Charles Varnas has convinced himself that he is immortal." He lifted the gun and examined it. "If that's true, then I will meet him in the lagoons of Lexington Avenue in five hundred years and we'll have it out. There can be no investigation, no witnesses. Not Wolfowitz, not Johansen. But now, I'm going to put the truth in your mind, so that you know the evil my daughter and Charles Varnas committed."

Kennedy saw it. "What have you done?"

"As for you, Kennedy…You're too clever, too good a bastard. I resent your goodness. You know too much, too soon, and too well."

"Christ—" For a moment, Kennedy appraised the space between them, the yard of cheap carpet separating him from the Adversary, that abyss that he would not be able to cross, to the enemy he could not kill. It was suicide to try. And yet, he must. Kennedy felt only the insult of the first bullet, not the cutting, nor the peeling, nor the slow sludge of the organs lain out on the bed—

CHAPTER TWENTY-FIVE

CONFESSION

MY NAME IS CHARLES Varnas. In the summer of 1925, I took a child into the desert surrounding the pyramid complex at Giza. The child had been with Campbell and me for the several months of our tour. It was, after all, our child. Almost five years old. Always, we maintained it in an adjoining room at whatever hotel we made our stop. I can still hear it weeping through the walls. I killed our child with a shaving razor that I dropped into the Nile River later that evening. I killed it.

Charles Varnas sipped his martini. "There. How is that?"

"Yes, it's good," Campbell said.

"Some moths believe they are birds." This was the phrase that found Charles Varnas as he blinked and opened his eyes, parting the shades of his apartment to the permafrost of Planet X. That was what Earth had become. Now they were to live with it, forever. Their building had been abandoned so long ago that he could no longer recollect precisely how it had been when others lived there, only the shadows of depression, the ghostly breadlines, and the floods, and the strange palm trees that had clung to the sediment banks of the streets, the dunes that had broken through the glass facades of the department stores and became smooth ramparts against the skyscrapers. From the banks of sand, tall red amaranth plants had risen like bloody antennae, reflected in the inundated avenues. The amaranth covered everything then, blooming from the mountainous sand, reflecting darkly in the dusky water. Campbell would travel in her gondola of reeds, drifting in her reverie through the empty city. It was an inter-regnum of muddy fertility, when giant herons stalked through the dreaming mangroves of Central Park, barely disturbing the water with their wading. Several small craft and probes had gone out from the high desert toward Bennu, the brightly glittering asteroid, before it struck Earth. It had been out there, waiting, screened from consciousness. He could not now recall the date of the collision that had brought the ice. Campbell might, he thought. He should ask Campbell. Everyone else was dead—

At least, with the confession made, he could write again. He could set the record of their ancient lives down. Fragments of poems, abstractions pulsed in his flesh and broke out upon the paper. The keys hammered their hieroglyphs upon blank white pages. Some time ago, he could not say how long, he had stood on the sand bank where the Chrysler Building leaned, shimmering metal like a rocket ship mirrored in the waters that had risen over the first two stories of the avenue. Swollen carp occupied the sunken lobby, pixelated light on the inlaid reeds. Adjusting his hiking pack, he felt himself being watched from far above. Where the accretion of sand had broken the glass and poured inside like the negative image of an hourglass, Varnas stepped in through one of the third-floor windows of the building with its aluminum birds flashing high in the sunlight. He found himself in a destroyed room, soft with decay, overgrown with crimson foliage. It might have been an office, he thought, feeling the rust on something that might have been a filling cabinet, but that now looked like porous reddish coral. The door was open to an unlit corridor. He removed his pack, located his flashlight, and drew his pistol from the holster at his ribs. With these in hand, he passed into the tower and began his ascent of the emergency stairs. North Africa, he recalled, was where the Bennu asteroid had hit, and the Nile had broken forever. His legs burned with the climb.

He had found Rafferty Oran Campbell on the 68th floor, in the red dining lounge with its mural of the city in the clouds. He wore a dark suit. Varnas' lost plague doctor's mask dangled from a strap at his chest. The sunlight flared through the window where Varnas and Campbell had taken their gin and watched the fading city, so many years ago. Varnas switched off his flashlight, and let it fall out the floor. It rolled away from him on the incline of the building. The floor sloped from the entry toward the glass like a surrealist painting. The granite pillars with their broken lights tilted within the shaft, meeting the cracked geometry of the ceiling. The man who had watched him stood and walked up the slope of floor toward him. Varnas stepped down. In the center of the room, they met.

"It is just as I told the detective: the murder of any child is a mortal sin, but worse, you killed your own child to deny me, a boy I loved." The Adversary exhaled. "A boy—that I—loved. But she, my terrible daughter in her skittering, stupid, panicked mind thought that I would occupy him like a hermit crab will a foreign shell. And she was absolutely bloody right. The son I should have had when she was born. It was she who occupied the hollows of the world where my antichrist should have been. The son I should have had, she had. I would have taken him back beneath my wing. I needed that boy."

"Rafferty—"

"You don't need your gun, Charles. I only want to know how she convinced you to do it."

Varnas did not hesitate. He lifted the pistol and fired. The first bullet hit Campbell's father in the throat, blowing a scarlet broth of larynx and bone from the back of his neck. The second took him in the steeping muscle of grief above and between his eyes. Rafferty Oran Campbell staggered backward, the penultimate spasms of his flesh carrying him toward the window. The large panes shattered and gave out under his torn shoulders, and the Devil careened into emptiness with his back studded with glassy plumage. Varnas watched him disappear. The corpse with the broken neck would find the reed broken water of Lexington—Five hundred years—The long fall—After the Crash—

"I say, it's good, Charles," Campbell said.

He did not answer.

"Charles?"

"I'm sorry, I was somewhere else."

"No one will ever see this, will they?" Campbell lamented. Crossing her legs, she lifted the typewriter into her lap, and stared at the confession, reading it over more than once.

"I don't think it means anything, unless we sign it before a witness."

"I think Kennedy might have understood it, in his own way." Campbell was agitated. "We denied the Devil his desire. Kennedy wouldn't blame us for that, even if the law said that we should go to the electric chair. It was, as he said, self-preservation. I could show him the tarot—the Devil with us chained before him—Truly, I think he might understand. Do you think someone will come here tomorrow? Do you think we should sign it if someone comes here, tomorrow?" Above the city, the stars seemed to falter for a moment, yet returned in the unpolluted night. "Charles, are we losing our minds?"

"I don't know."

"Let's go to bed," Campbell said.

He kissed her. He loved her as desperately as he ever had.

"We didn't have any choice, did we?" Campbell said.

"None."

They stared at the ceiling, blood racing. As he listened to Campbell's breathing, fitful shallows giving way slowly to an undertow of exhaustion, the palpitations of Varnas' heart were unremitting.

He watched the clock, and in two hours he had not yet slept. He ached for the Smith Corona but was afraid to wake Campbell with the tacks of his typing. He imagined the stars massed over the Nile, and the bed as a gondola of reeds. He saw Campbell drawing, plotting horoscopes on napkins at their first dinner with her father. He saw the crimson placenta on the white sheets. With infinite care, he shifted from the bed, and left her sleeping. He remembered having said, "What if we get up, look out of the window, and five hundred years have elapsed?"

Hoarfrost on amaranth—The winter of the planet—Five hundred years glimpsed through a frozen pane—Crimson amaranth plants beneath the snow like blood vessels under pale skin—Gondolas rotting in the risen waste of a crystalline cold—Stillness—A crater was named after Venetia Burney—Collapsing—When the meteor emerged from behind its screen—

Charles Varnas returned to the typewriter. At dawn a siege of beautiful giant herons passed between the buildings, casting a vast shadow on Central Park. When he had finished typing the rest of the confession, he and Campbell walked among the birds, as tall as they, and new inheritors of the world.

Because the Devil loved the boy. Perzival Varnas-Campbell, the child we called Percy was born on the edge of January 2nd and 3rd, 1921, in a room in East Hampton with a prospect of the ocean. Campbell said these were Hecate's days. Rafferty Oran Campbell had long abandoned the room after the death of his wife, and Campbell and I had taken it, shifting ghostly webs from the furniture, brushing moths into the grate. In her pregnancy, she would watch the starry water from the window, the spiring reeds in the dunes of the reaching beach, and the melancholy moonlight on the swell, as if it possessed some language absent from us. It was her mother's language.

The underworld in cold bloom—Heron tracks in permafrost—A pyramid's peak penetrating a white dune—The seas motionless and hanging with dead fish—Silent satellites—A gramophone trapped in a glacier—The last long longing of whales—An exhibit of moths under glass—

Rafferty Oran Campbell rarely brought himself to speak of his dead wife Lilith, and even to this hour, Campbell cannot trust her memories because she was too young. I have come to the point where I have no choice but to believe mine, whatever that means. I fill in what I can for Campbell, but there is really nothing I can do to help her that matters. I suspect that her father's wife was better than him, and yet, inadequate to him for being so. He envied her. He was afraid of her.

It occurs to me now, that giving birth to Campbell and her life was her mother's last gesture—not revenge, precisely—against him. I think of Campbell's small victory against her father at the grave by the Hudson in fresh light now, with the years behind us. And I recall laconically that night in Venice when I was beneath the Ascension dome. The Devil's daughter is ambivalent, and rebellious in a manner that—once more—he envied. Before we reached Egypt in 1925, he had lost us.

All the socketed stars—From crater to carrion cloud—And hoofbeat hills—The hollow cities—Cannibals chewing frostbit hanks under cold chandeliers—Burning trash in oil drums—Haunted department stores—All the money gone—Black skies and gunshots—

The birth of Percy, in that room overlooking the water, gave Campbell's father some belated hope. At first, I did not understand, but Campbell always knew. In that corrupted house, we dreamed of the exit. He set himself to the corruption of our child. I doubt that you can imagine how it must feel, how it absolutely has to feel to kill your child to protect it from evil. And yet, it happens every day.

Percy loved the beach. He loved the sand. Oh, God, if you could have walked that day into the dunes and let the evening come down upon you. Percy's blond hair was full of warm, new sand. I have been imitating it ever since. We walked for a long time and were happy. Percy was a good sport, and never complained as the day drew thin. As it was my birthday, in lieu of a cake we could share, I rewarded him with Egyptian pastries in sugared milk, and coin cakes of semolina. His blue-green eyes were filled with pleasure and curiosity. I held his small hand at the scaffolded Sphinx, and beside the pits where the star boats were buried, and through the ruins of the solar temples, and to the limestone and granite of the vast pyramids, sharp against the blue sky. I felt as though I was being crucified upon the anticipation of our grief.

A meteor casting clay across the sun—Towers of dirt thrown into the wind—Telegrams misfiring—Swollen lagoons of grief—Palms bending under snowfall—Hotels overrun with loneliness—The blast wave of Bennu—

Campbell could not stand it, and sickness drew against her in sweated sheets. If she could rise and leave the hotel—she had said—then, she would see me when it was over, at Khaled's Place, where Osman Raffi must have watched us. The tombs were cool, and dim, but Percy was not afraid of them. There were lamps, and ropes to lead us on the creaking planks, and he spoke in a small, eager voice about what he saw. At last, he was tired. With his last gay effort—he said I should carry him afterward—he put his hand in mine and we walked into the desert, away from the now distant palms of the suburbs and the tourist roads that connect life and death. As though I were native to it, I recognized the point when we were climbing the final dune. Upon that yellow crest of dust, the boy and I sat down. I drank from the Pernod bottle that I knew could never be sufficient to dull the pain of what would come.

Under the guillotine tide—The bending brine that broke the Sphinx—Dead trains at canal side—The jackdaw crypts—Crimson weeds over England—Currents of laissez-faire folding—

Percy lay on his back, breathless for the first time that day, surrendering to the alien fatigue that tightened his legs, and pulsed in his sunburnt brow. His breath and mine, the only sounds on that empty sea. I told him about the afterlife, about reincarnation, and immortality. He listened without asking questions. He was too tired. I think that—in the end—the sound of my talking to him was reassurance enough, after the incomprehensibility of his young life. I spoke to him about his mother, and about love.

Venice congested with corpses—Saint Theodore—The dragon stopped under his heel—Two columns—A winged lion—Napoleon's snub horse—The coral of a comet's tail—

The perpetual conflict that hangs, wings, and pins every childhood came to its crucible there in the awful desert. The Devil had made such offers. And we had spurned them. The sun was warm on Percy's eyelids, lowering them against his will. Lie down, I said. It's better. When he was still, I put my hand into my pocket and touched the shaving razor, keeping the cruel hover of my weeping silent. I watched him, almost dreaming in the vastness of the sun, and my heart broke. He was dressed in khaki shorts, and a white shirt, gray socks and brown monk strap shoes. I thought of the soft bulges of sand that must have gathered under his toes and heels. Then, I lay beside him and held his hand for the last time. His breath was sugared and steady. I whispered that I loved him and wished a happy birthday to all of us. The razor, impossibly heavy, was in my other hand as I leaned toward him. Somehow,

my despair broke. He heard the wretched, primitive sob that came
from me like an animal in a trap.

A sail-torn skiff rolls empty into ice floes—Death on the shore—
Two survivors walking—Mythologies collapsing—

The immensity of his reflection in the razor, I cannot consider.
As I felt, so Abraham must have felt. The exhausted boy lifted
his hands, at first only weakly against the scalding of the sun. But
this gesture turned in an instant to a defense against something
he realized in me, and he was terribly afraid. No! No! I thought
of Abraham at the summit of Mount Moriah, in the painting by
Caravaggio that Campbell had wanted me to see, *The Sacrifice of
Isaac*—The image that I would not remember five years hence,
behind her talk of Medusa, cut off, and alienated. The boy saw
himself elongated down the eternal blade. Abraham was prepared
to make his sacrifice, a blood-red robe falling from his aching
back—under what weight of future ghosts—his sackcloth shirt like
the color of the Franciscans at the breadlines—From the painting,
I recalled and hoped for the flaxen interceding angel with his dark
wings and finger of accusation and release. I saw the velvet ears of
the sheep—breathed the scent of lanolin—the animal's eyes antici-
pating the altar now that the boy was spared. The fix was in, and I
was one with the strange, disbelieving, defeated look in the father's
shadowed eyes—cheeks red from the scorch of the desert mountain
wind, from the bite of shame—as the angel grabbed for Abraham's
wrinkled wrist. Isaac's hands were pinned behind his back, dove
gray clouds massing over their distant home, where Sarah laughed.
Campbell's tarot card—The Devil—The two naked figures in
chains, Abraham and Sarah, now—Their child was screaming, his
head forced against stone by his father's dispassionate hand. I saw
that Abraham clung to the knife with all the baffled conviction of
faith. Abraham was old, the bones of his orbit stark, the hardness
of his face flowing into a tear-filled beard. I was a young man. And

yet, how different was I from Abraham in his delirium of sacrifice, and how remote was my child from his?

A bird hatching from the sun—A falcon from a stolen sky—A baby in a burning belly—A lifetime in an eye—

These are the skipping sounds of my dog-sleep nights. His hands and his wrists were so small, so pale and delicate that I could take both of them in one of mine. Tenderly, the shaving razor moved across the sweat-damp skin of his throat, where grains of sand stuck, brown and golden, yellow, and white. And the line of it became a slice, and then a gash that pulsed brightly, and soaked his shirt. He made no more sounds but twisted weakly for a few moments yet on the dune. I held his wrists gently, and then I held them not at all. And I did not know what I had done. Recollect the beat of wide gray wings. Because the Devil loved our boy. Because Percy loved the beach. Because he loved the sand.

Our little boy who returned to us as a meteor.
Our little boy who returned to us as a heron.

Campbell could barely recall what sand had been like. Charles Varnas struggled to describe it, as they walked the frozen white surface of Planet X.

ABOUT THE AUTHOR

James Reich is a novelist, essayist, journalist, and ecopsychologist. He is the author of the novels *The Song My Enemies Sing*, *Soft Invasions*, *Mistah Kurtz! A Prelude to Heart of Darkness*, *Bombshell*, and *I, Judas*. James is founder and publishing editor of Stalking Horse Press, and a contributing writer for *SPIN Magazine*. He is also the author of a collection of poems, *The Holly King*. Born in England, he has lived in Santa Fe, New Mexico, since 2009. www.jamesreichbooks.com

Printed in Great Britain
by Amazon